Other titles in the Chastity Riley series:

Blue Night
Beton Rouge

Simone Buchholz was born in Hanau in 1972. At university, she studied philosophy and literature, worked as a waitress and a columnist, and trained to be a journalist at the prestigious Henri-Nannen-School in Hamburg. In 2016, Simone Buchholz was awarded the Crime Cologne Award and was runner-up in the German Crime Fiction Prize for *Blue Night*, which was number one on the KrimiZEIT Best of Crime List for months. The next in the Chastity Riley series, *Beton Rouge*, won the Radio Bremen Crime Fiction Award and Best Economic Crime Novel 2017. In 2019, *Mexico Street*, the latest in the series, won the German Crime Fiction Prize.

She lives in Sankt Pauli, in the heart of Hamburg, with her husband and son. Follow Simone on Twitter @ohneKlippo and visit her website: simonebuchholz.com.

Rachel Ward is a freelance translator of literary and creative texts from German and French to English. Having studied modern languages at the University of East Anglia, she went on to complete UEA's MA in Literary Translation. Her published translations include *Traitor* by Gudrun Pausewang and *Red Rage* by Brigitte Blobel, and she is a Member of the Institute of Translation and Interpreting. She has previously translated Simone Buccholz's *Blue Night* and *Beton Rouge* for Orenda Books.

Follow Rachel on Twitter @FwdTranslations, on her blog www.adiscounttickettoeverywhere.wordpress.com, and on her website: www.forwardtranslations.co.uk.

MEXICO STREET

SIMONE BUCHHOLZ
Translated by Rachel Ward

**ORENDA
BOOKS**

Orenda Books
16 Carson Road
West Dulwich
London SE21 8HU
www.orendabooks.co.uk

First published in German as *Mexikoring* by Suhrkamp Verlag AG, Berlin 2018
This edition published in the United Kingdom by Orenda Books 2020
Copyright © Suhrkamp Verlag Berlin 2018
English translation © Rachel Ward 2020

A catalogue record for this book is available from the British Library.

ISBN 978-1-913193-15-7
eISBN 978-1-913193-16-4

Typeset in Garamond by www.typesetter.org.uk

Printed and bound by CPI Group (UK) Ltd, Croydon CR0 4YY

The translation of this work was supported by a grant from the Goethe-Institut London

For sales and distribution, please contact info@orendabooks or visit
www.orendabooks.co.uk.

MEXICO STREET

for Carrie Fisher

Every night we met at the fence.
We fell asleep
and held each other's hands
only in the morning I had a
deep furrow in my wrist.
But they've pulled down the fence
and they've built a wall there now
and every night I stand by the wall
and I beat my bones
on the stone.

—*From* Jesse James and Other Western Poems *by Franz Dobler*
Translated by Rachel Ward
Reproduced by kind permission of the author

ONLY A MULTI-STOREY

Do you remember the tunnel? That endless, long stone hole?

Course I remember. We walked through that tunnel so often.

If anyone had caught us, whoa. I was scared that every time a car would stop, someone would see us, one of your brothers maybe, and then there'd be massive trouble and all the rest of it.

Huh. Bullshit. I was invisible.

But you were worth loads, all the same. Fifty thousand at least.

They wouldn't even have got thirty thousand for someone like me.

Anyway. The way I see it now, I was just a golden goose to them.

At least they saw you.

They didn't even know who I was. And now I'm the guy who no longer exists.

So? I'll be killed if they find out where I am.

Sorry. Sometimes I'm an arse.

Hey, no you're not.

Can I hold you?

Too bright here.

Anyhow, the tunnel.

What about the tunnel?

I keep thinking about it.

Why?

Well, because I always thought that one day, I'd really be able to walk through it. From school to kung fu and then just not go home. Just walk on to the station. And get away.

Which you did.

I might have got on a train at the station, but I never really went anywhere. I'm still in between, I'm still in that tunnel, and it's dark in there.

Don't be so melodramatic. In the end there's a way out of the tunnel – there's a way out of every tunnel, and then there's the light.

As if you were anywhere. You know better than I do that it doesn't work like that. Hell, even the light yawns when it sees me now. The light knows damn well that it can't do anything with me anymore: he's never getting out of there. I swear the light's laughing at me these days. Like that scrap of light at the end of the tunnel over there, I can hear it laughing from here.

That isn't a tunnel. That's just a way through, under the car park.

Whatever.

I've got to go.

See you tonight down at the harbour?

Don't know.

OK. Well, I'll be there anyway.

OK.

Otherwise, back here first thing tomorrow.

Otherwise here, first thing tomorrow.

Promise?

Promise.

MAYBE ONE DAY PLASTIC BAGS WILL BE BETTER THAN GULLS

It's as if the buildings are breaking over people. One, two, puke: big chunks, everyone dead. A couple of architects on speed wanted to play Tetris against each other, and then everything got out of hand. Brutal boulders in washed concrete and steel stand around the place; they were white once, in the sixties and seventies of the last century; they used to gleam, but now the light is peeling off in great flakes.

There are cracks everywhere.

In between there's mirrored glass, merciless. The few open windows might also be smashed or broken or be missing in some other way, you never know exactly what's caused the black holes in the façades. The streets are canyons, and although lonely trees and brave squares of grass have been planted here and there, this is no place for any kind of life.

Lying at my feet, in the middle of a heap of fallen plaster, is a sky-blue lighter; it strikes me as sad and comforting in equal measure; I pick it up. The warm wind whirls a plastic bag through the air, and a second flies behind it. Maybe one day plastic bags will be better than gulls after all.

Sometimes I hold fast on to things that just drift past like that; it postpones facing the big stuff a little, but of course it doesn't mean I don't have to deal with the thing I'm here for, so I shove the lighter into my trouser pocket and the flying plastic bags out of my mind, and approach the almost-dead man in the half-carbonised car.

It was one of those early-morning calls that send you out on the trail without a pause for breath. Could I head over there? A burning car. Again. Apparently we really need to get a grip on these burning cars.

I'm not particularly interested in the burning cars. You know exactly why your cars keep burning, Hamburg.

But this time it wasn't just a car set on fire. There was also a person. Setting people on fire in cars – bugger that, it's not right.

I went without coffee, just slipped hastily into my boots and then into a taxi. When I reached the north of the city, a fireman was cordoning off a wide area around the scene of the fire. He said that the black Fiat hadn't been ablaze for long, they'd got here quickly. They'd been busy in this neck of the woods anyway because, you know, every morning since last summer there've been cars burning round here left, right and centre. The cheek of it, and besides, sheesh, our lovely cars.

'Yes, yes,' I said, this car business gets on my tits.

'...And this morning' – he just kept on talking – 'they were burning here in City Nord.'

But there are fires all over anyway, I think as I stand around, still a bit out of sorts because I'm so knackered. Everyone keeps getting worked up about the fires, and everyone keeps getting worked up about the helicopters searching the city for hotspots at dawn. Obviously you can't help hearing them, but they shouldn't be getting worked up about the helicopters, or about the burning cars either. They ought to be getting worked up about the things that cause people to set stuff on fire. The anger, the rage, the stupidity. We close our ears to it as if we could muffle our brains at the same time.

The fire has only affected the front of the Fiat; from behind the car looks almost new. But there's still smoke inside it, the poison must have crept in through every crack.

The driver's door has been cut open.

'Was the car locked?' I ask the emergency doctor who's kneeling beside the man on the asphalt, getting ready to insert a drip. His colleague pumps oxygen into the unconscious man's lungs.

'All the doors were locked,' says the doctor. 'And I was a bit surprised that he didn't call for help, given that everyone carries a phone these days. Or that he didn't just open the door – that's usually possible, isn't it?'

'Perhaps he was asleep,' I say.

'Perhaps he was drunk,' says the doctor, and it sounds like an accusation.

'But he'll survive, won't he?'

Shrug. 'I can't say. Depends how long he was in there for. And on the exact mixture he inhaled. The fire brigade say they were here ten minutes after receiving the call, but of course the car will have been burning for a few minutes before that, so you never quite know.'

'What are his chances?'

'After twelve minutes in the smoke, not so good.'

The man on the stretcher has one of those faces that look older than they are. Finely cut features, heavy stubble, but his skin looks soft and smooth, his eyebrows and lashes are thick and dark. He's not even thirty. His black curly hair is almost chin-length.

He's wearing a dark suit, not particularly expensive-looking. They've ripped open his pale shirt so that they can revive him quickly if necessary. That doesn't seem to have been needed yet, though, so his heart must still be beating.

All around us is dawn.

'The guy's got a good constitution,' says the doctor, standing up. 'Pretty strong.'

To me, though, he looks delicate, but I don't say that. I can't even think it properly, I'm afraid that the mere thought could weaken him.

He seems to be taken care of for the moment – the drip is in; the oxygen mask is on. Two paramedics carefully raise the stretcher and push it into the ambulance.

'Where are you taking him?' I ask.

'Barmbek hospital,' says the emergency doctor.

'Thanks,' I say.

The doctor gives me a somewhat perplexed look and says: 'Don't mention it.'

Then they drive off.

IT'S STILL NOT REALLY DAYTIME

The CID are here too, taking care of the car.

'Presumably it was the old classic,' says a young cop in a black shirt and a grey flying jacket. 'Firelighter on the front tyre and away we go.'

His short, stray-dog-blond hair lies on his head with an air of bewilderment; some of it is even pointing in a different direction altogether. He looks at least as tired as I am – he's either on the nightshift or he's only just fallen out of bed.

Come on, I think, let's get a bit more kip.

Right here, just lie down on the street.

Close our eyes and get away.

He stands there valiantly.

Holds a small folder out to me.

'The car documents were in the glove compartment. You should have a look at them.'

'What's up with them?' I take the papers.

The pilot-policeman tries to focus on me. It won't work. I'm fundamentally out of focus at this time in the morning.

'The name,' he says, not giving up: he's still looking into my face and concentrating hard.

I can't help him out there, though, so I leaf through the file. The Fiat Punto was registered to a Nouri Saroukhan in 2014.

'Oh,' I say. 'Saroukhan.'

'Uh-huh,' says the policeman.

I stare at the folder in my hand, the cop stares at me for another few seconds, I still won't come into focus, for Pete's sake, and then he seems to get fed up with it. He looks slightly miffed: his mouth turns down, as if he'd asked me a very important question and not got an answer.

'Did you find any other papers on the man?' I ask.

'We haven't searched him, the doctor wanted to get him stable first. The papers aren't going to run away.'

I nod, can't take my eyes off the name Saroukhan, and say: 'Could you call the Barmbek hospital right away? If the man has any papers on him, get them to stash them away for us. If that really is Nouri Saroukhan, this business might be rather bigger than it seems.'

I press the folder of car stuff into his hand. Then I pull out my phone and call Stepanovic, because I reckon that this will definitely be of interest to him. I could have called the organised-crime squad directly, but Stepanovic is something of that sort anyway, and we haven't talked for a day or two.

He picks up quickly, after the second ring or thereabouts, but then has a highly ostentatious coughing fit. He says he's at home and he'll get cracking ASAP. But when he briefly stops coughing, there's retro music and a young woman's voice fluting in the background.

I explain what it's about and exactly where he needs to come, then I hang up without saying goodbye.

At home, my arse, I think. Idiot. It doesn't bother me if he's formatting his heart with some woman, he can clown about with anyone he likes, and wherever he likes, for all I care. What annoys me is him telling me he's at home when I know that he never goes home at night. He only goes home in the daytime.

And it's still not really daytime, the light is only just creeping over the horizon. Stepanovic better not start taking the piss, not now we're friends or whatever we are.

My colleague from the CID has hung up too and is giving me that confused look again.

I know it's a bit much so early in the morning, and it is early, but hell, young man, that's how it is when you meet old ladies at ungodly hours, old ladies who can't sleep and are always, always tired. Then they are just out of focus and then they might not have had any coffee and then they're always easily pissed off.

But, of course, he can't help that.

I uncrease my brow, defrost my expression and look at him. The kid is really horribly dishevelled. Something's come along and taken him apart, but perhaps it was just last night. He looks away from me and at the phone in his hand.

'They've found his papers at the hospital,' he says. 'Nouri Saroukhan, German citizen, twenty-eight years old, born in Bremen, currently living in Eimsbüttel in the Grindel high-rises.'

'OK,' I say, 'thanks.' And I attempt a smile that probably looks as though I've got drawing pins in my mouth. 'Did they find a phone?'

He shakes his head. 'The doctor I just spoke to said he didn't have one on him.'

No phone.

Locked doors.

Most likely not a mistake then.

'So,' I say, 'don't talk to any strangers in the next ten minutes and take good care of things here till Chief Inspector Stepanovic from SCO44 gets here, OK? I'll go and get some coffee.'

A nod, the corners of his mouth twitch quietly.

As I go, he calls after me, says it would be great if I could possibly bring cigarettes too. I raise my left fist in the air and stick up my index and little fingers.

This cub hasn't quite got his head around the old vixen he's working with as of today.

DYING IN HAMBURG

There's no functioning café to be found in the wilderness of high-rise offices at this time in the morning, but I've got hold of a twenty-four-hour kiosk. There are various trashy papers lying in heaps in front of the till, and then there are the super-serious, grown-up newspapers people hide their tabloids inside. There's a shelf of sweets and a shelf of crisps, there's a fridge with beer and lemonade and stuff, there are endless cigarettes, and behind the counter there's a fully automatic coffee machine with any number of buttons. But there's nobody who could sell or serve me any of it.

'Hello?'

Again: 'Hello?'

Nobody there.

I walk out of the door and light myself a cigarette. I'm surrounded by insurance companies, but that doesn't necessarily make me feel any surer.

I feel a bit sick. The idea occurs, not for the first time, that in future I should only start smoking after nightfall; but three seconds later I abandon the idea, smoke the cigarette at least halfway down and go back in.

'Hello?'

Still no answer.

Fine. Then the prosecution will just have to brew her own.

According to my observations over the last two decades, you just have to press a couple of buttons. I tank up four paper cups of brown brew, one after another, without anything going wrong. If only everything in life was this easy to fill up.

I put twenty-five euros on the counter, leave the shop with two boxes of cigarettes, a lighter and the full cups on a cardboard tray and make my way back to the burnt-out car. A cherry tree drops its last petals as I pass. Even the wallpaper's coming down. Out of the corners of my eyes, on either side, I see office-worker prisons.

The Fiat stands in a cast-concrete clearing behind the multi-storey car park, the ground floor of which is more like an underpass, and parked at the end of this semi-tunnel is the brown Mercedes belonging to Ivo Stepanovic. Both car and chief inspector have seen better days. One has sagging eyelids and the other has sagging headlights. But when it comes down to it, everything still works.

Stepanovic and the young police officer have cigarettes in the corners of their mouths and their hands in their trouser pockets. So the kid isn't afraid of scrounging off the old man. Stepanovic is scanning the crime scene, his tired colleague is talking to a second detective: I'd evidently been too tired for him because I hadn't even noticed him till now. He is now holding Nouri Saroukhan's vehicle documents in his left hand. He holds out his other hand to me as he sees me coming with the coffee, but only takes the tray from me.

'How kind of you to get coffee for us all.'

OK, he's boring me already.

And I haven't got anything like coffee for us all, because another two officers in uniform have now arrived and are cordoning off everything that the fire brigade have already cordoned off, before taking a whole heap of photos. I can't decide whether to apologise for the missing coffee or duck away. Stepanovic settles it for me.

'I know the team.' He's slipped over to me and is speaking quietly. 'That guy only drinks tea. And the other can have mine.'

'Thanks,' I say, and I've immediately forgotten the phone routine from earlier. Over the last six months, Stepanovic has become a reliable solver of problems great and small, and you can forgive that kind of person a lot. I walk over to the uni-formed policemen with the two remaining paper cups.

'Machine coffee?'

'Thanks, that's nice of you,' says one, 'but I had litres of the stuff at the station last night – any more and I'll keel over.'

The other says: 'I'm a tea drinker.' And he twinkles as if we were on breakfast TV.

'Yes, no,' I say, 'uh, then ... that's fine.'

They carry on doing their stuff with mind-boggling levels of motivation. I rejoin my plain-clothes colleagues, press a coffee into Stepanovic's hand, and he takes it gladly after all. The deep furrows on his face suddenly soften completely.

'Sugar for anyone?' I ask, digging in my coat pockets. 'There wasn't any milk.'

The young cops watch Stepanovic and me with mild revul-sion as we stir far too much sugar into our coffee. They take hasty sips and lick their lips as if the gnat's piss tasted of any-thing but metal and cardboard.

We remind ourselves: fully automatic coffee machine. Button-pressed by me personally.

'So, Saroukhan,' says Stepanovic.

'Right,' I say. 'Saroukhan. Your colleague here picked up on that.'

'Very good, Rocktäschel,' says Stepanovic, clapping the young man – who is apparently called Rocktäschel but whose name I completely forgot to ask – rather too vigorously on his narrow shoulder blades. The coffee slops over. 'Interesting family.'

'Interesting family from Bremen,' I say.

'Exactly,' says the guy I find so boring. 'So why the hell are they suddenly dying on us here in Hamburg?'

'Hey,' I say, 'nobody's died here yet.'

'Give it a rest, Lindner,' says Rocktäschel, getting his smoke in his own eye.

I look at him, discreetly blow the smoke away and say: 'I can't help wondering: the name rang a bell with you so quickly ... but the Saroukhan clan's patch is a long way away from Hamburg.'

'I grew up in Bremen,' he says, stepping from one foot to the other and shivering slightly.

'You a Werder fan then?' asks Stepanovic.

Rocktäschel looks at him, and his neck muscles tense under his flying jacket. He throws the cigarette away. 'Is that a problem?'

All Hamburg sees HSV everywhere, and you really have to wonder how they managed to cling on for so long when they were serving up such dross for years.

Stepanovic holds up his hands and puts his head on one side. 'Hey, I'm from Frankfurt, no worries.'

'Pff, that's not much better,' says Lindner, probably because he wants to say something too. He earns himself a look from me, but as a straight right to the chin.

'Watch out,' says Stepanovic quietly. For a moment, everyone thinks he's still talking about the football; it takes a moment before we realise that it's about something completely different. 'Don't look now, just carry on.'

'What's up?' I ask quietly.

'There's someone on the car-park roof, watching us. A young woman. Flaming red curls. We'll keep talking, I've got my eye on her. When I give the sign, you all look too.'

Stepanovic is capable of seeing things from the corners of his eyes that other people wouldn't notice even if they hit them in the face. It's one of the skills that got him to SCO44. All the guys there have a dead-straight CID career path – obviously – as well as something special in the mix. They're interrogation specialists, techies, extremists of the senses. Stepanovic has eyes like nobody else, and he can immediately classify the stuff he sees.

We talk somewhat erratically back and forth, and I fidget about with one of the fresh cigarette packets. It's always extremely difficult not to look when someone's just asked you not to look now.

'Now,' says Stepanovic.

We turn our heads towards the car-park roof.

I'm just in time to see the fiery red hair as it vanishes below the parapet.

'Go,' I say to Rocktäschel, as I reckon he's the sportiest of the three men here, and I press my coffee into Lindner's hand.

Instantly, Rocktäschel is wide awake, for the first time this morning, but hey, it's at the right moment. He drops his cup, and we run together towards the car park entrance.

'You take the lift, I'll take the stairs!' he hisses to me, and we do it that way, but when we reach the roof, there's no red hair anywhere to be seen.

'Crap,' he pants, his hands on his knees.

'Too many options,' I say, looking around. The low concrete walls to the next-door buildings are easy to climb, she could have fled anywhere.

We sprint round every side of the roof, and check every possible escape route – nothing.

She's got away.

I stop for a moment and stand at the edge of the car-park roof, on the corner of Mexico Street and Überseering, and take a look at City Nord from above. What a crime to house people here, I think, how could they, and then my phone rings. Stepanovic.

'That was a woman who knows how to get away,' I say, and Stepanovic says: 'Nouri Saroukhan is dead. The hospital just rang the station.'

LET ME SPELL IT OUT FOR YOU, LINDNER

Stepanovic has organised a large, bright office for us on an upper floor, immediately between his colleagues from the SCO and the organised-crime squad. The light that comes in from outside is almost dazzling; a North German morning in early summer can sometimes have a hint of Scandinavia about it. The four of us sit around a large table, Rocktäschel and Lindner, Stepanovic and me.

'You were the first on the scene,' he says to the two younger guys. 'I want you on the team. And,' with a glance at Rocktäschel, 'I need you too, for Bremen. You must know your way around there pretty well, huh?'

Rocktäschel nods cautiously; something about the business seems to unsettle him.

Stepanovic writes our names on a sheet of paper and rests his right hand on my forearm, but only very briefly.

'Have you spoken to the attorney general's office to see if you're staying on the case?'

'I have,' I say. 'I am.'

He nods, leans back and looks at me. 'Which of the murder guys shall we bring in?'

'Are we sure that it was a murder?' asks Lindner, chewing on a pencil and looking clever-clever. Someone must have told him that it's vital always to chew on a pencil if you want to be listened to.

'Hello?' says Rocktäschel, looking at his partner as if he's had about enough already. 'Someone had clearly locked the car, the key's not there, Saroukhan didn't have his phone on him – whoever set fire to the vehicle was at least prepared for the chance that the bloke inside it would die. It's manslaughter at least, with a generous helping of malicious intent on the side. And I was on the phone to the hospital a couple of minutes ago, so, let me spell it out for you: Nouri Saroukhan was fit and healthy and had been stabilised to the point that he really ought to have survived the smoke inhalation. Something must have weakened his body prior to that. And if he'd been conscious when the car started to burn, he'd have got out. If he was only drunk and too soundly asleep, it wasn't murder. But if some-body put something in his drink or whatever, because he wanted to make sure that Saroukhan wouldn't make it out of the car, then it all starts to look a bit different. The body's with the coroner.'

He presses his lips together and gives his colleague a dirty look.

Lindner takes the pencil out of his mouth.

Stepanovic takes a deep breath and starts again: 'Which of the murder guys shall we bring in?'

I reckon we ought to start by establishing whether it's really such a good idea to have Rocktäschel and Lindner working to-gether, but, hey, I'm not the one putting the squad together, so don't mind me, suit yourselves, boys. Don't come crying to me if there's trouble.

'My choice would be Calabretta and his team,' I say, 'or else whoever's on call right now.'

'Will you ring Calabretta for me, then?' asks Stepanovic. 'I'd be happy to have him on board.' He writes the names

Calabretta, Schulle, Brückner and Stanislawski on the piece of paper in front of him.

'Will do,' I say, roll my chair over to the corner and pull my phone out of my coat pocket. Out of the window, the early May sun is shining on the rooftops of the city.

It almost makes me dizzy.

Calabretta's rather surprised when I tell him what it's about, because I haven't been in charge of a murder enquiry for ages. I tell him that it's more him who's in charge and that we're starting off by seeing what the hell is going on. He says that he and his guys will be with us in five minutes.

When I hang up, Rocktäschel's grabbed a thick blue pen and written the name *Nouri Saroukhan* on the large whiteboard on the wall at the head of the table.

'We still need someone from OC, don't we?' he says.

'I'll do for organised crime for the moment,' says Stepanovic, 'that's close enough. What we do still need, though, is a line to Bremen.' He stands up, grabs his leather jacket, his cigarettes and his phone. 'I'm popping out. I'll make some calls.'

'OK,' I say, 'so I'll bring the murder guys up to speed in a moment. Rocktäschel, we need the photos from the crime scene. Is there anything on the system yet?'

He puts the pen away and sits down at one of the two computers. 'I'll get right on it.'

'What shall I do?' asks Lindner.

I look at him and immediately feel so tired that I could drop off on the spot.

Man.

'Somebody ought to get hold of a coffee machine for us.'

If we had a decent director, something would fall from the ceiling with an almighty bang about now.

PRETTY GREY IN THE FACE

Calabretta, Stanislawski, Schulle and Brückner are here. It's really nice having the four of them so highly concentrated into this space. It's a kind of security for the soul. A backup copy of how things used to be. We're like a window that life has kept jumping through in recent years, and with every jump we've gone flying through space like shards of glass, but, because the shards know where they belong, they piece themselves back together, bit by bit, every time. Make a new window that, here and there, might be less than perfectly smooth, and that has certain spots that really need cleaning, but somehow you can see through it anyway.

The murder squad have taken their team desks in next to no time, these guys are total pros – a real pop-up shop. Schulle and Anne Stanislawski are welded to their phones, Calabretta's attached to his laptop. Brückner's writing the stuff his colleagues on the telephones and computers are finding out, piece by piece up on the board. There's now a vertical line under the name *Nouri Saroukhan*; to the right of the line it says:

Uni Hamburg
Studied law (dropped out)
AKTO Insurance (current employer)

To the left it says:

Saroukhan clan
Bremen
In Hamburg too now?

The left-hand side is the building site for Stepanovic, Rocktäschel and Lindner, and probably me too, while the right-hand side is for the murder squad, at least to start off with, for the first few hours, the early days. Then we'll chuck it all together.

Stepanovic has been on the phone and has clearly chain-smoked half a packet, he's pretty grey in the face and holding on to the door frame. His shirt crumples. Sit down, I think.

He nods to the swarming murder squad. 'Welcome on board.'

The murder investigators all briefly raise their hands and nod, but don't exactly look up. Anne Stanislawski is the only one to raise her eyes too, twizzling her strawberry-blonde, frizzy curls between two fingers. Three deep furrows have formed among the freckles on her brow; she presses her ear hard to the receiver and murmurs something down the line. Schulle has been wearing his blond hair with a surprisingly accurate parting lately, and he reacts only minimally to Stepanovic's presence. Brückner seems to want to learn what he's written on the board off by heart and, unlike his colleague Schulle, is in urgent need of another haircut; he looks like an ageing surfer boy. Calabretta does back up his nod with a jovial smile, but it's more kind of inward, because he too is all telephone.

The main thing is, he's here and that's good.

'Running like clockwork,' says Stepanovic, who likes to have work exactly the way it's coming along now. No fuss, just focused. 'Have we got a coffee machine yet, by the way?'

I look at Lindner, who blushes because he didn't arrange a machine, and is instead trying to assist Rocktäschel with sorting and printing the crime-scene photos by just sitting next to him.

'Oh, Lindner,' I say, 'you could have really made an impression there. What a pity.'

He looks at me, there's something throbbing at his temple and, I think, at mine too. Life with some people seems hard enough, but others make it even worse.

Stepanovic has noticed, he positions himself beside me.

'OK, people,' he says, 'play nicely. We're driving over to Bremen today; the guys over there say we can come. Lindner, Rocktäschel – head home and pack some stuff, we're staying a few days.'

He looks at me. 'Are you coming too? It could be interesting.'

Calabretta glances up from his computer and says: 'It's fine, feel free to just sod off, we've got everything under control here. Bit more phoning and then we'll leave too and get outside.'

I say: 'All right, Calabretta, right back at you.'

Then I go and pack.

THE VOID NEXT DOOR

The concept of coming home was never really my thing, but since the flat next to my flat has been fundamentally changed, it almost torments me to be at home. If at all possible, I'm not there. And if I am there, I try not to think about everything that isn't here, or rather I try to think about nothing at all. Just swallow the thoughts down; if necessary, something cold from my fridge can help with that.

The fact that Klatsche doesn't come knocking on my door at night anymore has made my flat a very quiet place. I swallow my thoughts down, and the void next door eats the sounds up, and every feeling along with them.

It's hard to sleep in the silence. In fact, it's impossible.

I always used to be quite fond of sleep.

Yes.

So.

Pack some stuff.

Packing stuff means that we're about to go away somewhere, and going away helps with some things.

I take my leather bag out of the wardrobe. Put clothes in it. Bathroom stuff. The bag isn't even half full.

I close the bag and then the door behind me; the flat next door scratches my face as I walk past, but I make it out to the street, and I'm standing there now, smoking and waiting for somebody to turn up finally and take me with them.

A short time later, we're sitting in Stepanovic's brown Mercedes, reasonably well dispersed, yet still rather out of sorts. Rocktäschel and Lindner are in the back, I'm sitting in the front next to the driver, because I always feel sick if I sit in the back for too long.

'The A1 needs repairing,' says Rocktäschel, then he falls asleep.

Lindner tries to involve Stepanovic in a conversation, but he puts the radio on. The woman reading the news says that this morning cars were burning in Hamburg, Hanover and Braunschweig, and so were a few others in Rostock, Berlin and Leipzig, and then nobody says another word; I drift in and out of a doze and stare vacantly out of the window. After an hour and fifteen minutes, we're in Bremen's Vahr district, turning into the grounds of the police headquarters.

A somewhat run-down brick building, which has had a bit added here at some time and a bit taken away there some other time.

At first glance, I reckon it's pretty well suited to us.

YOU CAN'T JUST RING THEIR DOORBELL

'Fritz Baumann, hello,' says the policeman who meets us at the door.

He shakes everyone by the hand, looking as though he's making a note of our names in his head. But in any case, he looks like he could make a mental note of everything, this shirt-sleeved kind of guy with wise, pale-blue eyes and white-blond hair that's just on the cusp between blond and white, just one tiny step more and it'll have made it. Baumann seems to be someone who makes a point of paying attention to everything, because everything is essential.

After greeting us, he shoves his hands in his trouser pockets, takes a step back and studies us. It's a little uncomfortable for us, but I can understand why he does it. Sometimes I'd like to do that too: start off by getting an overview of new people at my leisure, even if the new people might find it a bit odd. But I'm not so good at withstanding this-is-getting-weird-now looks anyway.

Baumann evidently withstands them pretty well.

Eventually, he's finished scrutinising us.

We take off our jackets and coats. It's mild in Bremen, the air is a little softer than in Hamburg. I'm slightly surprised by that.

'And?' asks Baumann, which is, after all, always a good question.

Stepanovic straightens his shirt, which has slipped halfway out of his trousers on the journey, and stuffs it back in again.

'We need to inform the Saroukhan family that one of their relatives has died,' he says, 'which presumably won't be that easy. Or can you just ring their doorbell?'

'You can always ring,' says Baumann. 'It's just that nobody will open the door. But I'll send someone with you to act as the door-opener.'

Interesting, the way these two alpha beasts immediately prowl around each other. I keep seeing that in Stepanovic when he meets other chieftains. A friendly, but very precise sizing-up.

Baumann sizes back. 'Nouri Saroukhan then.'

Stepanovic nods.

'As far as I know,' says Baumann, 'he was no longer one of the family.'

Stepanovic raises his eyebrows and, inwardly, all our mouths drop open for a moment.

'But we'll get to that.'

We shut our mouths with a snap.

'Of course, we still have to take them the news of his death.' Baumann looks Rocktäschel in the eye. 'I feel like I've seen you before somewhere.'

Rocktäschel straightens his back, I reckon it's more like he's straightening up his armour.

'Lennart Rocktäschel. My father was a colleague of yours.'

Something twitches in Baumann's face, first on his forehead and then around his mouth. He walks over to Rocktäschel, lays his right hand on his shoulder and glances in our direction.

'Come into my office. And phone a hotel. I think you'll need to stay a few days.'

Lindner pulls out his mobile and hunts for available hotel rooms.

Rocktäschel says he'll stay at his mum's. What a killer trick: staying at your mum's.

MAPS ARE GOOD

We hang up our jackets, Baumann pushes two extra chairs up to his desk.

'There are no more, I'm afraid,' he says, 'someone's always stealing the furniture here.'

The office walls could stand a bucket of fresh paint, the carpet under my feet feels lacklustre and brakes our steps, and the desk is a little lower than is good for a big man like Baumann. I station myself at the window. Out there is Bremen, flat but not cowering. Stepanovic and Rocktäschel sit down with Baumann. Lindner says he'll go and find some coffee, then.

'Right,' says Baumann. 'What do you know?'

'Bremen has a problem with Lebanese clans,' says Stepanovic, 'and the Saroukhan family are at the centre.'

'Not Lebanese,' says Baumann.

'Arabs?' asks Stepanovic.

'Not Arabs,' says Baumann, 'not Kurds, not Turks, not Palestinians.'

'What then?' I ask.

'Mhallami,' says Baumann.

'Sorry?' asks Stepanovic, and Rocktäschel looks fragile, sitting there on a large, rather shabby swivel chair.

'Mch-al-la-mi,' says Baumann. It's a real effort for me to grind the guttural sounds down into my brain. 'Like this,' he says, 'here, look.' He writes *Mhallami* on a piece of paper and hands it to Stepanovic, who immediately starts memorising each letter. 'Hard to pronounce, but you get used to it.'

Baumann stands up, fetches a large map from the shelf by the door and unrolls it on his desk. I come closer. Maps give me the feeling that I'm standing on solid ground. Maps are so good for me that I could stare at them for days.

Baumann's map is a map of the Middle East, someone's written *Mhallami Settlement Area* in the white margin at the top. Baumann takes a pen and points at a city called Mardin, in southern Turkey, on the north-eastern border with Syria. To the south-east is Iraq, to the east is Iran.

'This precise spot,' he says, as he pulls a pair of reading glasses from his shirt pocket and puts them on, 'around the city of Mardin, over territory that now belongs to four nation states, is where the Mhallami were settled by the Turks about eight hundred years ago. As mercenaries, as a kind of rampart against the Christian Yezidis. The Mhallami were a group of warrior tribes, they were supposed to protect this flank of the Ottoman Empire and keep the peace in the region.'

He takes the glasses off and leans back.

His brilliant pronunciation of the word *Mhallami* is driving me slightly nuts, but the main thing driving me nuts is the thought that it might soon be my turn to have to pronounce it.

'So technically we're not talking about criminal clans, or mafia families either, but ancient tribal structures, who were paid, over centuries, to perceive everything outside their structure as the enemy. Would any of you like to take notes?'

'I can,' I say. 'Has anyone got a pen and some paper?'

'Don't bother,' says Stepanovic, 'just listen up. I'll make notes in my head.'

I nod and think: *OK, boy*. Cos I know he can do that. This evening in the pub, he'll rattle it all off between beers.

Baumann fiddles with the glasses in his hands.

'As mercenaries, the Mhallami were the lowest class, they were the bottom rank, and never had any rights at all. There wasn't a state to protect them, and there isn't one to this day.'

'That's hardly unusual in the Middle East, though,' says Stepanovic.

Baumann looks at him as if he's butted in. Fair enough; he did. Baumann pushes the reading glasses back into his hair and immediately takes on a kind of directorial air, which rather suits him, then he keeps talking, without responding to Stepanovic.

'The nineteen thirties, the era of Turkification, when all the non-Turkish minorities were put through the mill, saw the first major wave of migration into Lebanon. So the Mhallami ended up as Kurdish refugees in the camps around Beirut.'

My gaze catches on Rocktäschel, who is staring intently at the map. Something seems to be giving our young colleague the wobbles.

'At that time, they were mostly working in slaughterhouses around Beirut,' says Baumann, rolling almost imperceptibly to and fro on his swivel chair. 'Hauling dead cattle. The most menial jobs. That poverty belt around the slaughterhouses was one of the first areas to be flattened by the Christians in the Lebanese civil war. Many Mhallami families fled to Europe right at the start of the war.'

'And checked in here as Lebanese refugees,' I say, at the risk that this time it'll be me butting in. 'That's why we talk about Lebanese-Kurdish clans, but that's incorrect.'

Baumann nods. 'Exactly.'

He seems a little more pleasant to me than to Stepanovic.

The door opens, Lindner comes in with five mugs and a Thermos jug of filter coffee. My stomach aches immediately.

'Oh,' he says, 'aren't they Lebanese then?'

If I had a desk in front of me, I'd drop my head onto it, but there's only my ribcage and although, as I've often noticed, it's toughened up over the years, it still isn't hard enough to pass as a desk.

Baumann looks at Lindner, without a flicker.

Stepanovic takes a deep breath and says: 'We'll go over it again this evening.'

That's not good enough for Lindner: he doesn't know how good Stepanovic is at paying attention.

'But what passports do they have then?'

I think briefly that it doesn't really matter a damn who's what, and what passports they have, and what are we talking about here for all this time? Passports, nationalities, good grief, we're talking about people; and there are problems. But perhaps it does actually matter. If we have to tell a mother that her son is dead, but we can't just ring that mother's doorbell as we're clearly a problem for her just because we are who we are, and because she is who she is, if we're enemies, then first of all I need to know why, and where it all started.

Don't I?

Or do I?

I mentally lob the question and my doubt about it out into the room, but unfortunately there are no telepaths present, so the question just bounces once over the desk, grazes the map and darts back at my throat, where it immediately sinks in its teeth. My hand reaches for the spot, and I notice that the question, and everything related to it, doesn't just bite, it has barbed thorns too.

Lindner focuses on pouring coffee and looks kind of screwy.

Rocktäschel continues to focus most of his attention on the map.

Stepanovic is focusing all kinds of glances on me, because we do actually manage a spot of telepathy sometimes.

Baumann stands up and walks across the room, he gets a big roll of paper from another shelf, he unrolls the paper with a flourish and hangs it on one of those flip-chart thingies that's standing there looking a bit lost. Drawn on the paper is a bizarrely interlinked, highly detailed family tree.

He walks back to his desk and sits down.

'Well, let's stop here for a moment, shall we,' he says. 'Because the answer to your colleague's question is complicated and describes the situation perfectly: these people are largely stateless. The Lebanese, for example, say: "They're Kurds or Turks, they're nothing to do with us, you can't shunt them off onto us." The Turks say: "They're Arabs, we're not taking them." And the Kurds say that too, and they don't even have their own state anyway. The Mhallami themselves say: "We're Kurdish-Lebanese", but that's actually a load of total bullshit that somebody came up with at some point.'

'So that means,' says Stepanovic, 'that most of the Mhallami came here without passports?'

Baumann nods. 'Some had Lebanese papers on them, travel documents called *Laissez-passers*. Those papers listed status, nationality, place of birth and profession as *à l'etude*, which pretty much means *under consideration*. In Lebanon they were usually known as "travellers through". And that's pretty apt. No passport, no secure status, only ever tolerated, could never get work permits, and most of them still don't have them.'

Travellers, I think, and Stepanovic says, in one of his fits of waistcoat-pocket-philosophy: 'Travelling through. Aren't we all?'

Baumann gets up and comes to stand beside me at the window.

'What do you think, then – who are these people?' I ask.

His face changes to something between tired and soft, as if he were hugging a pillow, and then he shakes his head very gently.

'My Mallami.'

He pronounces it differently now. Not in the semi-correct Arabic way that's the best European tongues can manage, but with a Bremen accent.

The way you say it when you've known each other a long time.

'In the early nineteen nineties, five federal states, including Bremen, Lower Saxony and North-Rhine Westphalia, passed "Kurdish Acts", he says. 'They said that we wouldn't send Kurds back to Turkey or the crisis areas in the Middle East, because they would inevitably end up between the frontlines. From that moment on, the Mhallami started arriving here with Turkish papers as Kurdish refugees.'

Lindner and Stepanovic pluck up the courage to try the coffee, Rocktäschel is warming his hands on his cup. Baumann turns towards the window, looks out and keeps talking.

'The reception facilities sent them by train to their next ac-commodation, but they generally didn't even arrive, preferring to go straight to join their families, where they underwent another rapid change of identity – having come from Frankfurt as Turkish Kurds, they checked in somewhere else as refugees from the Lebanese war and started a new asylum procedure. And suddenly their name wasn't Turkish anymore but Arabic.'

He turns back to face the room.

'Has anybody kept on top of all that?' asks Stepanovic, taking a cautious slurp of coffee while I send him incessant tele-pathic signals that he'd be better off leaving it alone.

'Well, that's what we spend most of our time doing,' says Baumann, 'keeping on top of it. For example, we know lots of families, with a total of five different Turkish surnames, who all just used the Arabic name Saroukhan to apply for asylum here in Bremen. And then they settled down here under that name. The family structures are utterly impenetrable, and that makes them ideal criminal structures. Besides which, each woman has an average of ten children, so there's no need to recruit members from outside, which gives a clan a certain measure of security.'

He points to the monstrous family tree on his right.

'If you draw up the family relationships, after three gener-ations, there are so many lines, there's just a black mark in the middle.'

I take a step closer to the family tree. Stepanovic stands up and comes over to me. He leaves his coffee cup behind.

In every generation, both the Arabic and Turkish names of most of the men are illustrated with little black-and-white photos from the police records department; very occasionally, we can see a woman too. Stepanovic narrows his eyes to slits and turns to Baumann.

'Could I borrow your glasses for a sec?'

Baumann smiles, and the smile holds, even in the moment when he takes his glasses off his head and hands them to

Stepanovic. You see, boys. There we go. Stepanovic puts on the glasses and looks at the photographs. He points to the picture of a man in the grandparent generation.

'Is it possible that they all look like this guy here?'

'There's no getting married or having children outside the family,' says Baumann. 'According to the legend, that thickens the blood and strengthens the family. And it's convenient.'

'Why Bremen?' I ask.

'It's not just about Bremen,' says Baumann, 'it's just that it builds up here because, basically, a city state is a small space so everything builds up. There are maybe three thousand people in the Bremen families, and about half of them are known to the police. The name Saroukhan and a few other names can be found in lots of places in the north, and the whole of central Germany. In Berlin, in Lower Saxony, in NRW. Anywhere there was cheap housing in the nineties. And where there was business to be done.'

'What kind of business are we talking here, actually?' asks Stepanovic.

'Anything that brings in cash,' says Rocktäschel, who is now holding his hands over his coffee cup as if it were a dying camp-fire that just won't cough up any more heat, but he isn't giving in. 'Illegal gambling. Hiring cars, reporting them as stolen, then selling them. Fake policemen scamming old people on the phone, scaring them into leaving their jewellery or their savings outside the front door at night so you just have to go and pick them up. Forcibly setting up fruit machines in new pubs and cashing them up every week, but not without holding a few heads in cold sinks or against hot coffee machines. And all kinds of drugs, from crack on grubby street corners to cocaine in fancy restaurants and clubs.'

'Correct,' says Baumann. 'These gentlemen do absolutely everything. But we just don't usually have the time to deal with their criminal activities. We have our hands full containing the violence that spills out onto the streets from their internal quarrels and clan wars. And we don't even have the capacity for that. I'm sure you noticed the empty corridors in this building.'

Lindner leans back in his seat. 'I strongly suspect that your colleagues aren't just out and about,' he says.

'Correct,' says Baumann. 'My colleagues just don't exist. Jobs and money have been cut for decades. We're only just starting to train police officers again. Nobody's exactly fighting for a job here, though.'

He looks at Rocktäschel and his expression tosses something into the room that feels as though it'll explode if you even touch it. 'Now just imagine driving a patrol car through Bremen city centre.'

WITH GUN-SHOT WOUNDS

The night was darker than other nights, the clouds in the sky had arrived in layers and swallowed up all the light, the street lamps groaned, helpless against it. Along the Disco Mile, angular crimes against architecture towered into the black sky, and the music pounding from their ground floors sounded as though it was made of steel. Standing beneath the trees were helpless signs bearing the message that it's forbidden to carry weapons here.

Amid the metallic darkness, the trouble broke out like a monster. The monster smashed everything to smithereens – cars, windows, people, and at a furious pace, so fast that nothing and nobody could be protected. The exact cause of the trouble was almost irrelevant, the important thing was the trouble itself, because the trouble made the bang, the boom, that flung it all up in the air so that things came down in new patterns, so that there was peace in the end because, ultimately, trouble is only ever about one thing: who's the stronger one here, and who's weaker.

About sixty men faced each other, around thirty on either side. They had baseball bats, knuckledusters, nunchucks, guns. None of them was older than thirty-eight, the youngest was fifteen.

The blood flowed fast and in a variety of ways, it flowed from the backs of heads, from mouths, thighs, knees, bellies.

The police came with two patrol cars and four officers; the third car out on the streets that night was busy with domestic violence in another part of town, in Walle, and couldn't get away. Four policemen got out of the cars: one died instantly, the other three were taken to the nearest hospital with gun-shot wounds, one of them had made it back to his car and raised the alarm, but by the time the mobile operational unit arrived, the trouble, the smoke and the men had long since scattered.

Nobody could ever establish exactly who was involved or exactly what the trouble was about.

It had probably started with an insult.

THE MORE THEY YELL, THE LOUDER THE BANG

Lennart Rocktäschel is sitting on his chair and his top lip is trembling a little; he looks at me, and I ask myself, why does it have to be me? I get the feeling that he'd like to jump up and get out of here. I vacate my safe place by the window, murmur something about 'sitting down for a bit', pull the swivel chair that Stepanovic was sitting on as close to Rocktäschel's chair as possible, and sit down on it.

He keeps looking at me, the tremor in his top lip eases up.

'Some of the families are at odds with each other, if not actually enemies,' says Baumann, 'which is why we prefer to talk about clans these days.' He links his hands and flexes his fingers until they crack. 'About twenty people make up a clan, which is also generally very tight-knit, in everyday life too – they all live together in one house, for example. And there are regular rows between the clans. Mostly over trivialities: one clan chief's wife pushed in at the check-out in Aldi or whatever. But sometimes there's more to it than that. So there might be a redistribution of the drug business in the pipeline, or a general power-base expansion, or a marriage had been arranged but the deal didn't come off because another clan stuck its oar in, or whatever. Then, the queue-jumping will just be a pretext to stoke up all the emotions.'

'The more yelling they do beforehand, the louder the bang afterwards,' says Stepanovic.

'That's exactly how it goes,' says Baumann. 'And the banging was pretty loud around the millennium; at any rate the guys who were out on the street even back then put up their hands and said: Hello, Bremen, we've got a problem with organised crime, with a new, completely self-contained structure. It only took ten years or so for politicians to catch up. By then it was undeniable and the time for trying to talk it away was long past.' He turns back to the window and looks out over his city. 'Since then, we've been trying to catch up, and I swear our tongues are hanging down to our knees.'

TORCH IT

Sometimes, back when Rami wasn't yet a proper man, but so close to it, when his big brother kept saying he really ought to start shaving to make a decent beard grow soon, and he always thought, what exactly am I meant to shave? – there's nothing there, but OK, if it's important then I better had, he'd fetched his father from the tearoom because dinner was ready at home.

The tearoom had no windows, or at least none that you could look in through. Rami had sometimes tried to look out when he was waiting for his father to finish talking to the other fathers, but that didn't work either. The windows were wallpapered shut. There was nothing new about that, Rami was familiar with that kind of window, the windows at home were always kept shut somehow, papered shut, blocked shut, curtained shut. But now and then he thought that it might actually be quite nice to be able to look out occasionally. He'd never dared ask why the windows had to be blocked. He'd soon got out of the habit of asking any questions at all.

If you asked the wrong questions, you got a slap.

Now that he's a man, he's completely lost the desire to ask anything. Men don't ask questions, men give answers.

It's good that the windows are blind.

The ones in the tearoom, where his father still sits, day in, day out, and the ones in the sports bar that's his sports bar. For betting on football, and slot machines, for business and everything that needs discussing.

People who aren't part of the family very rarely come in, there's no reason for them to, and if they ever do, they leave again soon after. Because his brother Abdullah, aka Esholeshek, just stares them away with his meaty forehead.

Keep the hell out of here, says Esholeshek's brow.

Today they have to discuss the matter of his sister. She's supposed to be marrying Kadir, Rami's cousin. She's the fourth sister, Rami's the fourth brother, so he gets the dowry.

Problem: Kadir already has the sister.

But Rami doesn't have any money yet.

And Kadir fetched her a week ago.

Abdullah says that next month she'll be pregnant. By then, Kadir has to have married her and paid for her, for fuck's sake.

Still. At least she's finally gone. Not the most elegant, Rami's sister. And almost eighteen already. And she eats a lot, so she costs a lot of money. To be honest, Rami's been waiting for his cash for three years now, for three years it's been his turn to have someone marry his sister so that he gets the money for her, that's what she's for. His father says there's still thirty thousand in it. Two years ago, it would have been fifty thousand. Stupid cow. Why's she so fat?

Kadir comes in, with two brothers. They're wearing the shiny leather jackets that all the men in his family wear. Disco jackets. Shit jackets.

In Rami's family, the men wear baseball jackets and baseball bats.

Every arm tenses.

Rami's stuck his gun in his belt and his knife in his shoe.

He asks Kadir where his sister is.

Kadir says she's in his kitchen, cleaning. And at night, he says, she's in his bed.

But she's not that good, he says.

'Give me fifty thousand,' says Rami.

'I'll give you twenty thousand,' says Kadir. 'She's knackered already.'

'You knackered her,' says Rami.

Kadir laughs and his teeth look like pebbles.

Abdullah stands up from his place.

Kadir says Esholeshek needs to sit back down again.

Rami says nobody needs to tell his brother what to do.

'Twenty thousand or nothing,' says Kadir and spits on the floor. 'Think it over. I'll come round again tomorrow.'

He turns and walks out of Rami's sports bar, his two brothers leave too, and Rami's jaw is now as hard as a sword.

'Djamal!' he calls. 'Hussein!'

His two little brothers come out of the kitchen. Thirteen and fifteen, little big shots. Rami loves the kids, they're handy for anything. But if there are things to discuss, he'd rather they waited in the kitchen. You never know. At any rate, they can listen and learn stuff from there.

Now there's nothing more to discuss.

Now there are things to do.

'You know where Kadir parks his car at night?' asks Rami.

The brothers nod.

'Torch it.'

Later, just before eleven, the black Mercedes is up in flames, Djamal and Hussein have made a very good fire: hey, it wasn't their first.

A neighbour taking his dog out sees the car burning and the two boys running away. He calls the police. Just before they arrive, Kadir and his brothers arrive too, because: Man! My car's on fire! Who did that?!

I want to know who did that, says Kadir, while the neighbour's still alone with his dog, the police car's just coming round the corner. The neighbour says he called the police. And saw two boys running away.

Two boys, aha, says Kadir.

The police car stops, two policemen get out and try to clear up what's happened, and meanwhile the fire brigade arrives and they put the car out, and a few more people are coming now, they're all coming from the direction that Kadir and his guys came from, from over there round the corner on the left, and the people are talking even before they get there, they run up to the others, talking, and the more they talk, the louder it all gets, especially in the policemen's heads. The only people not talking are Kadir and the neighbour, but for different reasons. Kadir doesn't want to talk; the neighbour can't, he can't get a word in.

In the end, he can't even remember why he went out, the dog on its lead almost dissolves into the darkness, and he's also forgotten the two boys he saw skedaddling.

Kadir is relatively satisfied.

He'll sort out the rest in the morning.

Djamal and Hussein miss out on the whole crowd, they're seven streets away by now, and on the way home they take a detour through the Steintor Quarter. Rami will be pleased if they sell a bit of crack to the losers.

He loves how quickly they're learning.

Djamal's been in training with his brother for a year now, and Hussein for two. Your mother won't teach you any of the skills you need, their father tells his sons when they turn twelve, and then he hands them over to their big brothers. He used to train them himself, but he can't anymore, he's too old. And the boys know that they'll learn the important stuff better from Rami anyway.

Selling drugs, stealing things, stealing cars, driving cars, setting fire to cars. Nobody's better than Rami, he did it himself for years before he got his sports bar together.

Kadir storms into the sports bar the next day with two extra brothers, and a few cousins on the side, because Kadir is properly pissed off.

The men line up.

Rami and his three brothers in the rear of the bar, two cousins with their backs to the counter, the two little ones waiting in the kitchen as usual, with the phone at the ready in case it gets rough and Rami needs reinforcements. But the main reinforcers are in their pockets.

Reinforcers with silencers.

Mafia style. Cool.

Kadir stands at the door with eight men, hands down. More hands that could reach the guns in their trouser pockets in a flash.

They've been practising for moments like this for as long as they can remember.

Yesterday evening, when Rami sent the boys off to torch the car, he knew his cousin would turn up on his doorstep today, and he knew that he wouldn't come alone.

'I've got five thousand for your sister,' says Kadir, breathing like an ox. 'The other five's your deposit for my new car.'

'Your cars aren't even worth three thousand,' says Rami, and the bullet's already in his throat.

He falls.

The next to fall is Kadir's brother Omar; Abdullah – Esholeshek – was the quickest to react.

The air smoulders, and mixed in with the smoke is the stench of everything the two dying men let go of in the instant of their deaths.

Then there's just shouting.

In Kadir's flat, Rami's sister shuffles along on her knees, scrubbing the kitchen floor.

The matter never reached the police.

It was settled by an arbitrator who travelled in from Hanover. Ismail, an uncle of both the dead men, a man in an outsized suit with silver hair that collided with his collar at the nape of his neck. A hundred men from across the whole of northern Germany were at the negotiations.

The perpetrator-victim mediation was settled by way of money. Ordinarily, Rami's death would have cost a hundred thousand. Taking Omar's death and Kadir's bride-kidnapping thing into account, there was still 75,000 left for Rami's family. Kadir and Abdullah were banned from the mosque.

What would happen with Rami's sister was not discussed.

DON'T DO ANYTHING I WOULDN'T DO

Baumann sits back at his desk and rubs his face with both hands. 'I once spoke to a mother whose son was almost fourteen,' he says. 'If your boy carries on like this, I said, he'll get four years in juvie any day now. And do you know what the mother replied?'

'Don't give a shit,' says Rocktäschel.

'Precisely,' says Baumann. 'She said it would make a man of him. These people despise our civil society, and they're unimpressed by our legal system. They think we're weak, scared, petty and pathetic.'

'A mafia, innit,' says Lindner.

Baumann gives him a stern look, which, if you ask me, Lindner could do with in general.

'Mafias always infiltrate politics and the economy. The lads here are nowhere near that stage. They haven't even realised that the big money in Germany isn't made from drugs and small-scale dealing in stolen cars, but from VW. And at the moment they just don't have the access to the relevant levels of society, but they're just starting to, here and there. They occasionally team up with some lame-brain rappers who think they're gangsters, and then they hang around at parties or appear in a video. But that's it, it's not anything yet. So, mafia – no. We're dealing with a relatively recent and basic criminal structure.'

He picks up the telephone receiver.

'I'll call someone who'll take you to see Nouri Saroukhan's parents.'

After a while, he speaks to a colleague, calling him Fredo, who will presumably pick us up in a bit.

'DCS Bargfrede knows the family pretty well,' says Baumann. 'And I would recommend you don't do anything that he doesn't do.'

'Why was Nouri Saroukhan no longer part of the family?' I ask.

'We don't exactly know,' says Baumann, and suddenly there's a mournfulness in his voice. No idea who or what he's mourning, Nouri, the Saroukhans, the impotence of his office. 'We only know that he was cast out.'

'Wow,' says Lindner. 'Medieval.'

'How does a thing like that happen?' I ask. 'Being cast out?'

'It usually happens when somebody defies the family,' says Baumann. 'As you know, Nouri Saroukhan went to Hamburg in 2009 to study law, and his father won't have funded that because his son felt like it. If it turns out that one of their many kids is intellectual enough to pass their exams and go to uni, they always study dentistry or law, depending on their grades. But you need such high grades to get into dentistry, they'll more likely study law, so any uni candidates are always kept carefully away from anything criminal.' He looks at the clock. 'In this city, we've got plenty of dentists and lawyers from Mhallami families.'

'Clever,' says Stepanovic. 'That way, expensive services are kept in the family.'

'Which means they're free from then on,' says Baumann, giving him a brief smile – an almost appreciative smile. Probably meant to mean: *Neat trick, huh?*

'Maybe you'll be able to find out exactly what happened in Hamburg that led to Nouri being cast out,' he says. 'All our detectives ran up against a brick wall with their sources, and of course it wasn't important enough to pursue it what with all the routine stuff we have to do.'

He looks at the clock again.

'Bargfrede will be waiting. We should head down to reception.'

'OK,' says Stepanovic. 'I guess it would be better for three of us to pitch up than five, wouldn't it?'

Baumann nods. 'Just don't make too many waves. Who's going?'

Rocktäschel looks like he's had hours of being beaten round the head.

Stepanovic says: 'Rocktäschel, you can call it a day if you want. Go and say hello to your mum, I'm sure she'll like that. Riley and I will take on the Saroukhans. And Lindner, if you'd go and check in for the three of us at the hotel, the bags are in the Merc.' He dangles the car key in his face and looks around the group again. 'Shall we do that?'

I nod. Let's do that, dude.

'Do whatever you like,' says Baumann. 'I'll show you out now.' He stands up. 'See you tomorrow morning, about eight.'

You can see me about eight, I think, but I can't promise that I'll be able to see a thing.

LOOKING AT THE MOOD HERE, I'D RATHER STAND

Tim Bargfrede, a stocky guy of about forty, parks the police car in a side street in the Steintorviertel. We get out. If it weren't for the faint hippy veneer – a spot of subculture on a lamppost here, a little leftie politics in a window there – this would be a strikingly middle-class area. Classic nineteenth-century Bremen townhouses, painted in pastel colours, with little front gardens and rose arches and steps with wrought-iron railings up to the front door with a basement below.

Bargfrede stops outside a plain white house. A bit of grey stucco, brown window frames, the façade no longer immaculately maintained, but so far so good. No garden, there are concrete slabs at the bottom of the steps. Bargfrede walks past the steps into the yard and stops outside a low door in the side wall.

'It'll be best if you let me do the talking,' he says.

Stepanovic and I nod.

Bargfrede rings.

There's a dry floral wreath hanging over the door from last autumn.

'Yes, hello?'

The intercom. A woman's wavering voice.

'Bargfrede. Hello, Mrs Saroukhan.'

Hesitation.

'Wait there.'

Nothing happens.

Then a buzz, a click.

Bargfrede pushes the door open.

We follow him down a corridor, then through a moderately large laundry room in which there are three washing machines, two driers and a folded-up clothes horse.

A man is waiting for us at the foot of the dark wooden staircase that leads upwards.

He's leaning on a stick that he holds in his right hand. He's wearing black trousers, a white shirt and a dark cardigan. His hair, his thick eyebrows and his beard shimmer silver in the light of the bare bulb dangling from the ceiling.

'Mr Bargfrede,' he says, his voice rasps.

He looks at Stepanovic and me for a fraction of a second, scans to see if we're important, we're obviously not.

'May we come in, Mr Saroukhan?' asks Bargfrede.

Saroukhan says nothing, turns and walks up the stairs. He finds the walking difficult, every couple of steps, he takes a break. Bargfrede walks slowly behind him, keeping more distance than is usual on stairs. We, in turn, keep our distance from Bargfrede. The outline of his service revolver can be seen under his dark-grey windcheater.

Stepanovic takes my hand on the last four steps, squeezes it for three seconds, then lets go again.

The stairs lead us into a hall; the hall ends, in one direction, with the front door, which is hung with blue blankets; nobody seems to use this entrance for anything. A socket hangs from the ceiling but there's no bulb there. At the other end of the hall is the living room. Three two-seater sofas in black leather, a coffee table in the middle, thick white curtains at the big window that looks out over the back, lots of rugs, a display case with countless photos from the weddings of countless couples. On the couch sits a woman of Mr Saroukhan's age, so presumably Mrs Saroukhan. Standing by the window are two very broad men with identical haircuts, black pomaded hair, the sides almost shaved, but not quite. They must both be around thirty, but it's hard to tell because they're backlit by the sludgy light that gets through those almost-impenetrable curtains, and their solid mass makes it hard for me to think. As far as I can make out from here, they seem to be the spitting image of their father.

Nobody says a thing. Nobody offers us a seat, and looking at the mood here, I'd rather stand anyway.

'We have to bring you some sad news,' says Bargfrede, who makes no move to introduce us, so it's presumably better that way. 'Your son Nouri was found dead in Hamburg.'

The brothers don't move, they just look at Bargfrede.

'We are assuming criminal action.'

The mother tilts her head slightly.

The father stands there as if he's been encased in concrete, he supports himself doggedly on his stick, only the hand gripping the handle shakes a little.

Nothing happens.

Then: 'Nouri decided many years ago no longer to be part of our family. He became a stranger to us.'

His gaze travels over to his sons, who are standing in front of the thick curtains; it looks as though he'd like to look out of the window for a moment, but neither the sons nor the curtains are letting anything out or in.

'I have had no son called Nouri for a long time now.'

He breathes in once and out once, then the hand on the stick stops trembling.

'If you would kindly leave now.'

I open my mouth because I want to say something. Anything. It doesn't work like that. Their son is dead, what's up with the mother, why isn't she reacting to it, this can't be right.

This is wrong.

Stepanovic brushes my forearm very gently with his hand, I close my mouth again.

Bargfrede turns to us and says, quietly: 'Let's go.'

We walk out of the dark room, down the dark hall, down the stairs, the lightbulb flickers, the laundry room smells of fabric softener. I can't believe what's just happened here. I'd been expecting rage, shouting, tears, anything, but not nothing at all.

When the door clicks shut behind us and we're out on the street again, Stepanovic and I light up from a standing start and Bargfrede says: 'I don't really smoke, but can I have one too?'

After three or four drags, which we smoke in silence walking back to the car, he says: 'You just never get used to it.'

'I really don't want to drive back out here tomorrow to sound out their alibis,' says Stepanovic.

'No need,' says Bargfrede. 'The Saroukhan brothers, along with a good thirty other Mhallami men, spent last night in police custody. There was a massive bust-up between several clans. They weren't out until nine this morning.'

'What was the row about?' I ask.

Bargfrede shrugs his shoulders.

'Someone dropped a slice of cake, maybe. Do you want to pop back up and ask?'

No, I think.

I want to smoke.

GOTTA BECOME A GANGSTER

Rocktäschel's phoned. He's having dinner at his mum's and then staying right there. Stepanovic, Lindner and I are sitting in one of those burger joints that have shot up in every town in recent years, as if the future of the species depended on us eating tons and tons of mince. The men were desperate for a burger for dinner, they claimed that, otherwise, after a day like we've had, their brains would shrivel up.

'Shrivelled-up brains are the last thing we need,' I said, by which I mainly meant my own mental capabilities, and that's why we're here.

The place is OK, though, because the toilet walls are papered with old comics and you can also order plenty of food with no meat in it. In front of me is grilled halloumi with a spicy sauce. I can always rely on warm cheese to stick together some of the cuts inside me – temporarily at least.

Our table's by the window, it's too small, and it wobbles.

'Don't let it get warm,' says Stepanovic, taking a big swig from the bottle. I follow suit and so does Lindner, and I take note: so long as he doesn't speak, he's quite bearable.

In the meantime, it's got dark outside. Bremen, night. Students, skaters, ageing hippies, ageing lefties, civilised people. The wrecks are out among them, not in any greater numbers than anywhere else, but in this particular part of town they seem to be extra-focused on how wrecked they are, on every knock the world has given them along the way. They're pretty much in tatters, they declare as much at top volume, and Bremen somehow adjusts itself around them.

Various shady guys in slick and no less shady cars drive up and down the road, again and again: I see each car at least twice, three times. Souped-up bangers that, for all the noise they make are actually just mid-range Audis disguised as luxury models. The young men sitting in these wannabe-Ferraris sure as hell look similar to the two Saroukhan sons we saw earlier, standing at the thickly curtained living-room window.

'No shortage of gangsters out tonight,' says Lindner, and for once he's actually said something that I'd say if I were in the mood for talking. 'Don't they normally prefer taking care of business to standing out like that?'

Stepanovic bites into his burger, chews rather laboriously and watches a red, lowered Mercedes C-Class.

'They're just kids,' he says through a mouthful, chews again and swallows. 'They're up to here in testosterone.' He holds his right hand by his right ear and holds his beer bottle in his left. 'So they need to impress somebody several times a day, and it's a well-known fact that loud cars are pretty handy for that. Or that's what they think, anyway.'

He swigs some beer, so does Lindner, so do I, by which time the bottles are empty enough to order a second round. I send a signal to the barman; he nods and knows the score.

'But you can't impress the hippies out there with cars,' says Lindner. 'They don't give a shit about cars.'

Three young women are walking past outside, two of them have young men on hand, all five are wearing 1970s' gym shoes, and if they don't have challenging haircuts they have challenging glasses, but as a whole they're really beautiful, maybe just because they're so young. You can see at a glance what the women think about men in flash, noisy cars: Oh look, another couple of guys with tiny dicks.

It's not about these people, I think, it's about your own people.

'Their kid brothers think the cars are cool,' I say. 'That's enough.'

'Probably,' says Stepanovic.

Lindner knits his brows. 'You mean, like: if you wanna grow up cool and have a cool car, you gotta become a gangster like me?'

The barman puts three new beers on the table for us, we give him the empty bottles, and he says:

'That's just how they see it, people.'

NO TOUCHING

The hotel is on a four-lane road that seems much too big for the superficial cosiness of this city. But once we're standing in the lobby, it's quiet and peaceful again, the light from the turquoise lampshades pours a dark soup into my head. We take the lift up to the fourth floor in silence – not that we were talking much before. Lindner vanishes straight into his room. He's either very tired or he's sick to the back teeth of us. Stepanovic and I stand idly outside our doors for a bit.

'I'm not sure,' he says.

'What about?'

'If I should go in there.'

'Maybe we could get a peaceful night's sleep for once,' I say.

He looks at me and he looks like a ghost.

'Cos neither of us is having to hang in there at home, you mean?'

'That kind of thing,' I say. 'I'd like to give it a try.'

'OK,' he says, and gets right up close behind me so that the two of us are outside my door.

'Ivo,' I say, 'oh, man.'

'I'd like to give it a try too,' he says.

'But not that,' I say.

'No touching, Riley. But also, no being alone. We can have

a drink from the minibar, I'll bend your ear with my shit, and at some point, we'll fall asleep.'

I turn to face him and look at him. His thick, grey-flecked hair frames his lightly furrowed face, his black eyebrows make the mud-coloured eyes look darker than they are, his expression is working hard to reel the situation back in; right this second, it's slipping away from him.

'That won't work,' I say, but I'm not entirely sure about that. Perhaps the idea is one of the best in years. No touching. Just talking. And then finally sleeping.

I feel as though I haven't slept since twice forever.

My exhaustion and a room without a void next door are tugging at me, and both want to have me all to themselves.

'Sorry,' I say, slowly shaking my head. Then I turn around, hold the key card to the lock and I'm in.

It's so quiet I could scream.

I pull my coat and boots off, I open the window wide and sit on the windowsill, right next to the sky. I light a cigarette and I'm basically only waiting for the same thing to happen next door in Stepanovic's room.

But he's obviously forgotten how to smoke, or he's dropped dead of heartache, or he's just not there.

After I've spent ten minutes staring alone at the sky, I realise that I'm not going to be able to sleep. Dammit, I should have brought him in.

Serves me right.

You can't just let friends starve outside your door.

I stand up, pull my boots on again, get my coat off the hook and leave the room. As I head for the stairs, I meet Stepanovic, walking towards me.

'Hey?' I say. 'Were you coming to see me?'

He shrugs his shoulders. 'Nah, but as you're here … Um, I went for a bit of a walk, just round the corner here there's a bar, they've got twenty-three kinds of gin.'

'OK,' I say, laying my hand on his chest.

He gives me a cautious grin.

He knows I'm on the hook.

I pull cigarettes out and stick one in each of our mouths.

'But let's drink something slow.'

TWENTY-THREE KINDS OF GIN ARE TWENTY-THREE KINDS OF GIN

The May sun beams over Bremen; Stepanovic and I are sitting in the car, waiting for Lindner, who had to nip back to the loo. Calabretta's on the phone, on speaker. He's on the move somewhere outside, I can hear the city rustling in the background. The first investigation results from Hamburg are in.

'Nouri Saroukhan's flat has been turned inside out and sealed. Funny place, by the way, forlorn, makes my Spartan pad look like a fairground. You two ought to have a look at it when you're back. Stanislawski and I are just off to AKTO Insurance, to sound out Saroukhan's colleagues. Schulle and Brückner are heading to the uni to talk to professors, lecturers, secretaries and former coursemates. Hang on a moment...'

He addresses two sentences to someone else and then he's back.

'Anne says forensics just rang. Our victim had GBL in his blood.'

'Roofies,' says Stepanovic. 'Well, well.'

'Yeah,' says Calabretta. 'It was planned.'

Stepanovic hangs up as Lindner pulls open the door behind my seat and hurls himself onto the backseat with a curt 'ready!'. The Merc shakes, my brain vibrates. File under: twenty-three kinds of gin. We did drink slowly, and in the end each of us fell into our own beds, or at least I think so, I can't quite remember, because in the end twenty-three kinds of gin are twenty-three kinds of gin.

Lindner is dressed to the nines; he already was when we met in the lobby half an hour ago, but now he must be up to about ten or something. I run my hands over my face and then my fingers through my hair, although a proper face is a different thing altogether, and I'm further than ever from orderly hair. Stepanovic does the same thing with his three-day stubble.

Ach.

Come on.

Let's go.

Stepanovic starts the Mercedes, and we get on the road to the police HQ as cautiously as our condition demands, nice and gently along the Weser for a bit, then turn off left into the Vahr district, the car radio singing away to itself, and so is Stepanovic: *Whatever I'm thinking about right now, my thoughts always come back to you*. Last night cars were burning in Cologne, Düsseldorf, Dortmund and Bochum, as well as in Stuttgart, Munich and Augsburg.

Lindner says it's weird we've got such boozy breath, we didn't drink that much beer yesterday, hey, he's fine.

Sweetie-pie.

You just walk a mile in my shoes.

NO LOVE

The porter waved us straight through to Baumann's office, and he's sitting behind his desk again, legs spread wide, reading glasses on the tip of his nose.

'It's half past eight.'

'Sorry,' I say, and don't elaborate further – what else should I say? Stepanovic and I flooded our brains last night? Lindner needed the loo again?

Baumann's expression says: it's all the same to me, let's get started, there's lots to do.

Rocktäschel has clearly been here a while, I really wouldn't have expected him to be the up-with-the-lark type. He's rolled up his sleeves and he's fiddling about, trying to put up some kind of screen on the wood-chip wallpaper. Baumann's computer is linked to a projector and is in front of the screen, which is now finally up and might even stay that way. There are four chairs.

Rocktäschel straightens the screen up again and looks at us. His face looks as though he's spent the whole night skinning his brain.

'Good morning,' he says, 'I've been setting things up.'

'Good morning,' I say, and I try to smile at him. It actually seems to work.

We sit down.

Baumann says: 'I'll show you a bit of the material that we've officially filmed, and a bit of the stuff that a colleague regularly fishes out of the Net.'

'So where are the fish biting right now?' asks Stepanovic.

Baumann takes a slip of paper, writes a name and a phone number on it, and holds it out to Stepanovic.

'Ms Schäfer herself is the best person to tell you that.'

Stepanovic stands up for a moment, takes the slip, pockets it and sits down again.

I don't reckon he'll call her. He's the kind of guy who doesn't actually care where the stuff on the table in front of him comes from. Food, drink, music, women, information: the main thing is, it's there.

Baumann stretches his left arm out a bit and presses a switch by the door, the shutters roll down outside the windows. It's not dark in the room, but dim enough that I could drop off on the spot.

Watch out.

I hear Baumann click something on his computer and now here we go.

'So, a bit of TV to start with,' he says. 'This is the opening credits from a historical series about the warrior tribes in the Kurdish settlement areas. Very popular with my Mallami. Just so you can get an idea of the kind of world that goes down particularly well with them.'

Desert.

Sand.

Sun.

Horses.

Superimposed lions' heads.

Then there's a roar and everyone goes for each other, with

machetes and swords and other kinds of killing devices and loads of pathos on infinitely many male faces. Eventually the intro's over, and then the history starts, and at first it carries on in exactly the way it began.

'The way they see themselves,' says Baumann. 'Basically nothing's changed since then.'

'Bloody noses all round,' says Stepanovic. 'An interesting concept, of course.'

Baumann nods in the half-light of his office. 'Survival of the fittest, the weaker goes to the wall. And now have a look at how that gets expressed in the families.'

A click, and here comes the next film.

A small boy, he's maybe nine or ten years old, he's wearing combat trousers, his upper body is naked, he has his hands crossed over his chest, his fingers are pretending to be guns. He's leaning on the bonnet of a silver Mercedes, rapping into the camera.

'... *hey Berlin, watch out, we're all in the house, we'll do what it takes, we're the brothers, Berlin, you limp dick, eat this, Bremen's in the house, Berlin, you piece of...*'

It's followed by heaps more incomprehensible, fucked-up stuff. The clip is maybe thirty seconds long, but that little boy, making guns with his hands and obviously threatening some load of gangster colleagues in Berlin, weighs down my lungs. I mean: he's a kid.

Click. Next film.

'This is Abdullah Saroukhan,' says Baumann. 'He's known as "Esholeshek", which means "son of a donkey". He's pretty much the muscle. He's been arrested and the police records department are trying to photograph him.'

The man in the film is wearing a vest and a blue baseball

jacket with a gold emblem, an S with a kind of laurel wreath around it. The man is asked to hold still just for a moment and look into the camera. But he doesn't, not for a second. He thrashes continually, he's furious, he swears at the officers.

You can hear a quiet voice in the background, someone's trying to calm him.

No chance.

After a while, the man goes for the policeman behind the camera, the others try to subdue him, then the film breaks off.

Click. Next.

'House search in Östliche Vorstadt here in Bremen,' says Baumann, 'filmed on bodycams.'

It gets straight down to business. Heavily armed police on the stairs in an old building, running upstairs, male voices can be heard from above. Lots of shouting. The police get to the top floor, facing them are young, broad-shouldered guys in T-shirts and joggers, every single one of them armed with a knife. The yelling continues, now the police are yelling too. It's loud, it's intense, it's hard to see what's actually happening. In the end, every male family member is lying, secured, on the floor, the part of the search team that isn't kneeling on anybody is passing through the flat at a run. It's all more like a martial-arts computer game than a house search.

'I can't believe they're all so aggressive,' I say, looking at Baumann. 'I mean, all of them?'

'The guys are all on the ragged edge when they go into a Saroukhan house now,' he says. 'Things have gone wrong too often, in that kind of direct contact, there've been some pretty big bust-ups.' His voice drops, he glances at Rocktäschel, who's sitting with crossed arms and knitted eyebrows. 'And that's what the Mhallami are used to, the boys learn young that in a conflict that's how you act towards anyone who isn't part of your own group: aggressive and brutal.'

'Works great,' says Rocktäschel, his expression unmoving as he speaks. 'I experienced it first-hand in primary school. Obviously for those boys, me being a policeman's son was the biggest possible provocation. All those times I got beaten up by their big brothers for some little thing. All those times they started with anyone who wasn't the way they wanted them to be. Eventually I stopped counting.'

'There are people from some parts of the Middle East,' says Baumann, 'who are mystified by all our fuss about humanism and respecting the rights of the individual, they don't give a stuff about it, they don't even know what the hell it is, it doesn't exist. In their world, it's the collective that matters; the tribe, the family that's important. The individual person, one man, one woman, one child – feelings, needs – none of that has any great value, nobody has ever learnt to consider it. So there's no sympathy for what happens to one individual. Here, for example, you can get a really good view of what that means for the people who are born into these families.'

Another click, the next film starts.

A party.

'A wedding,' says Baumann. 'Have a closer look at the two blokes in the background – the one on the left is the bride's brother, the one on the right is the bridegroom. Do you notice anything?'

Two young men, standing facing each other, looking at each other, their eyes razor-sharp, but they're not really meeting each other's eyes, they're looking past each other. Both faces are carved in stone.

'They don't like each other,' I say.

'They hate each other,' says Baumann, 'they've taken knives to each other, even shot at each other. Their last meeting put one of them in hospital for three weeks. But they're about to have to dance together. Just because custom says so.'

The men take each other's hands and start to move to the music. Forwards, back, forwards, back, towards each other, apart, and every time they dance towards each other, there's the hint of a kiss.

'That's crazy,' says Stepanovic, 'no way. I'd explode. Are they from enemy families? And is the wedding meant to make peace, or what?'

The two enemies seem to dance on forever, grinding their jaws, while they blow those sodding kisses. It's just torture, I can't look and I stare out of the window. The sun is shining as if it were high summer, at least here in Bremen.

'At that time, the families were actually getting on fairly well,' says Baumann, 'there wasn't really any trouble to pacify with a wedding, the aggro was just between those two men, for whatever reason. Besides, Mhallami weddings are more about business than politics. The bridegroom pays between thirty and fifty-thousand euros to the bride's older brother, depending on the value they put on a girl. How pretty she is, how young, how many children the women in her family have on average, so how much child benefit there'll be. Done. It's about cash.'

'So he could look a bit cheerier,' says Stepanovic, pointing to the bride's brother.

'He could,' says Baumann, 'but that's not his style.'

At last the guys' dance is over. Click. Next film.

A very young girl in a white lace dress, she's been painted with so much make-up that she looks in her early twenties.

She's staring into space, seems to be waiting for something she finds uncanny.

'Same wedding?' I ask.

Baumann nods and says: 'Watch. Here comes the bride's mother.'

A woman in a claret-coloured and much-too-shiny dress appears on screen from the right. In silence, she starts decorating the bride. With a veil, with jewellery, with flowers. Mother and daughter look past each other exactly like the two dancers just now.

Reminds me of a visit from my mother. It was a few years back: there she was, forty years after she left me, on my doorstep. Because she hadn't wanted to be alone at Christmas. I'd looked at her in a pretty similar way.

'No love,' I say.

'Just coldness,' says Baumann.

We then watch another two films of that wedding. One of the bride being handed over in return for money, followed by a short sequence at a large table, as there's eating. Jumping around beside the table are two small boys, maybe seven or eight years old, who suddenly start fighting, but it's not just some playground scuffle, it's really brutal. They're punching each other in the face, kicking each other in the stomach, one of them headbutts the other on the nose, the nose starts bleeding. The adult men around the table are entirely unbothered. They don't even react, they just keep eating as if nothing's happening.

Click, next film.

'Last film,' says Baumann. 'A meeting of various family heads. We suspect it took place somewhere in Lower Saxony, but that's just speculation, because unfortunately we weren't there.'

Filmed from above. A heap of grey heads. Then the camera zooms in, the film gets a bit fuzzy but you can still make out the faces, mostly at least.

'This was probably filmed secretly,' says Baumann. 'Some person who thought there was something in it for them stuck a camera up on some hidden hill or perch, and then put the video on the Net.'

The men with grey hair are standing in a group, talking. They're in a clearing, all around them is not particularly dense forest. Younger men are walking through the group, handing out tea. There's no sound, you can't hear anything, but the faces under the grey hair speak volumes: this seems to be serious.

'What's it all about?' asks Stepanovic.

'Meetings like that usually happen when there's a major con-flict to resolve,' says Baumann. 'Maybe someone got killed. Maybe the son of one family shot the son of the other family, for example. These meetings are about how much the culprit's family has to pay the victim's family to put an end to the thing. You see the group in the centre? The four silverbacks in the middle there?'

Four older gentlemen who look a bit more serious and a bit more important than the rest.

'Those are the arbitrators,' says Baumann. 'They virtually replace our legal system. You'll see their scorn for people like us this afternoon. Bargfrede has ordered Nouri Saroukhan's parents to come here so we can grill the family again.'

He stands up, winds the shutters back up and switches off the projector. Suddenly, everyone looks very tired, not just Stepanovic and me. For a moment, the room fills with such a huge sense of helplessness that it almost creates a vacuum.

I take a deep breath and notice that I'm still here.

Baumann stands over by the window, and with the light behind him he looks even taller than he already is.

'Did you notice anything about all the faces?'

I have no idea what he's getting at, the vacuum's pulled the plug on my brain. Too many pictures that threw up too many difficult questions. I feel a bit sick.

'They all look so serious,' says Stepanovic.

Baumann nods. 'Exactly. Nobody laughs even once.'

True, I think. Not even the children laugh.

'The Mhallami world is a quintessentially humourless one,' says Baumann. 'The means by which many social groups, whole societies even, defuse or even resolve their conflicts, i.e. humour, doesn't exist in that system. It just doesn't happen, rather like in the Italian mafia. Perhaps that's why we, with all that we are, are bound to run aground there. Because we're missing a very important shared tool for communication.'

And none of us can laugh at that either.

It's like a punch in the belly.

Baumann looks at the clock.

'So, in two hours, the Saroukhans will take to the field here, probably a whole squad of them. Do you want to get something to eat first?'

Lindner nods, Stepanovic too, I'm not hungry but I follow them to the canteen. After all, I'm world famous for my sociability.

SHITSHOW

After the meal in the canteen, we didn't go back to Baumann's office, we landed up in this conference room, for we are many. Baumann, Bargfrede, Stepanovic and me, Elmedina and Ismail Saroukhan, and their sons Ali, Hamsa and Mahmud. Hamsa and Mahmud are the two we met in the Saroukhans' house, but they didn't give any sign of knowing or recognising us, and their parents react in exactly the same way.

Stepanovic and I are thin air. Rocktäschel and Lindner wait outside. Rocktäschel mumbled something to himself, he couldn't do something, I didn't catch quite what, and Baumann immediately signalled that was OK, and anyway, it'd be better if there were only four of us. File under: keeping an overview.

The old Saroukhan sits in the middle of the family, resting his hands on his stick. He's thrust out his chin and knitted his eyebrows, and he's grinding his teeth, which makes unpleasant noises and sets his silver beard trembling slightly. He could equally well be the patriarch of a Bavarian village.

His wife sits beside him, making herself small.

The sons have set themselves up on chairs around the edge, the young men's shoulders are so broad that they can't do up their blue baseball jackets.

Bargfrede takes charge of the conversation.

'Mr Saroukhan, it looks as though your son was killed. He was drugged and set on fire.'

Silence.

'Any idea who might have anything to do with it?'

Silence.

'Was Nouri still in touch with any of your family?'

Silence.

'When did you or your wife or your sons last speak to Nouri?'

The silence keeps getting louder.

'Would you like us to find your son Nouri's killer, Mr Saroukhan?'

The old man looks at Bargfrede. 'You know perfectly well that I have no son called Nouri.'

Then his face falls back into silent rigidity.

Bargfrede presses his lips together for a moment. Like he said: you never get used to it.

'You already lost a child a few years ago, Mr Saroukhan.'

Who? What?

I look at Baumann first, then Stepanovic, but neither reacts.

Ismail Saroukhan's face darkens even further, I wouldn't have thought it was possible, but he manages it. And although he's not tall, and he's definitely no giant when sitting down – he looks more like a seated square – he looks down on Bargfrede.

'Do not dirty the legacy of Younes Saroukhan with your questions.'

It was more growled than spoken. He squeezed it out between his teeth.

'What legacy?' Bargfrede stretches, and now he looks down on Saroukhan. 'Illegal car races? Brawls? Drug dealing?'

Saroukhan breathes audibly out and in again, but he holds

himself back. He doesn't flip. It wouldn't be good for the family if he flipped now. He can flip better at home.

'Do you know what I don't understand, Mr Saroukhan?'

Bargfrede must want to keep getting on his nerves.

'Whatever quarrels you have within your own family, don't you even want peace? I mean, you come here from war zones, you can have a good life here on your child benefit, why don't you live in peace? Why do you keep on stirring up these private wars?'

Saroukhan leans forwards in his chair, lays the hand that isn't resting on his stick on the table and looks at Bargfrede as if he's about to bite him.

Bargfrede holds his gaze, Baumann is serenity personified, only Stepanovic looks nervous. He isn't happy about all this stuff, I can tell. I'm not happy about it either.

Saroukhan flattens his hand harder on the table top. 'I don't want your peace, policeman.'

'It isn't my peace,' said Bargfrede, 'it's our peace. We like it.'

'You are worms.'

Now Bargfrede also lays his hands on the table. He takes a deep breath and bites something back.

'One day your children will stop playing along, Saroukhan, and then we'll see who's the worm here.'

The detective chief superintendent is talking like a mafioso, but it suits him.

Saroukhan leans back again.

Bargfrede really is as cool as fuck. I don't think he's blinked for about a minute. And he just keeps going.

'When did you last speak to Nouri?'

No answer.

Bargfrede looks at the brothers, one at a time, and asks each of them: 'How about you?'

He does it because he has to. He doesn't do it because he expects answers.

Lastly, his gaze rests on Elmedina Saroukhan. She ducks her head between her shoulders. He doesn't even ask.

Ismail Saroukhan stands up laboriously from his chair and sniffs, which sounds no less laborious. Such an effort to be here.

He looks first at Baumann and then at Bargfrede. Then he raises his stick and draws a circle in the air.

'We are leaving.'

His wife and his sons stand up.

Now I can't help it, now I have to say something, I'm just not cool enough.

'You don't actually give a shit what happens to your children, do you?'

I have to be careful not to spit at him, I'm so irate.

'And where were you on the night Nouri died?'

Saroukhan looks at his stick, then he turns his lowered head a fraction back towards his oldest son and growls again.

Ali Saroukhan looks a whisker past me, but his gaze is meant for me, I can sense that, because it feels as if someone were peeling my chest with a sharp knife.

'My father doesn't talk to women.'

Stepanovic lays a hand on my forearm and says: 'Will he talk to me then?'

He only says it to annoy Ali, to annoy the old man, actually to annoy everyone, I know that, and I appreciate it.

'No.'

Ali Saroukhan points to Baumann, who has made no move to join in with the conversation at any time.

'From now on, he will only talk to him.'

'Well now,' says Stepanovic, 'that really is silly.'

Baumann and Bargfrede look reproachfully at him: how daft are these colleagues from Hamburg? Man, man, man, maybe we'd have got something out of them.

But we're not buying that one, guys.

And the thread of Stepanovic's patience is snapped anyway.

He stands up, takes two large steps towards the door and slams it behind him with a loud 'This shitshow!'

I keep thinking that there really could be something amazing between us.

BREMEN NEEDS BATMAN

'We're heading to the Litfass,' Rocktäschel said as we stumbled out of the police HQ with our heads down that evening. Baumann had shown us a few more films and told us how Nouri Saroukhan's younger brother came to die in a car crash in 2013. He'd said that it wasn't an accident. Younes Saroukhan's car was forced off the road and crashed head on into a container during an illegal motor race at the port.

The investigators met with a silence that spread throughout all Bremen's Mhallami families about everything to do with the accident. It was impenetrable, and the car that forced him off was untraceable; the death of the youngest Saroukhan offspring is unresolved to this day.

So now we're sitting on barstools in a line along a long bar in the Litfass: Lidner, Rocktäschel, Stepanovic and me. The yellow light is gradually patching us up, hour by hour, and by now, so much beer has flowed through us that not even Lindner is annoying.

We're barely talking, but we're smoking a lot to make up for it – now and again, someone growls something. Stepanovic has his hand on my knee, but then he likes to do that sometimes, it doesn't bother me, it's his way of keeping in touch with the outside world when he bows out and turns inward and thinks. He only takes the hand away when he says something and at some point – the fog around us is pretty thick by then – he says: 'Rocktäschel, what exactly happened to your father?'

I'd never have dared to ask that question so clearly, but the elephant's been in the room since yesterday, and at times today it was so big that it barely fitted into Baumann's office. It was squishing us all against the walls.

Rocktäschel stares at the beer pump. 'Gunfight on the Disco Mile,' he says, '2006. My father was sitting in one of the first two police cars to arrive.'

I catch the barman's eye, raise four fingers on my left hand and say, quietly, 'Vodka.' The barman fills that many empty glasses.

'He took two bullets. One here,' he puts a hand on his belly, 'and one here.' He touches his left temple.

'I'd just started a physics degree. But after my dad bought it, I joined the police instead. In a fit of romanticism.'

Stepanovic lays his hand on his back. It's no good, the sadness spills out everywhere.

We take the vodkas and pass them on.

Rocktäschel and I were the same age when our fathers were killed by guns, except that my dad pulled the trigger himself.

Rocktäschel raises his glass. 'People from port cities always have hope,' he says, and I think, where's a port around here, huh? Then we all raise our glasses and drink, probably to our fathers.

The Strokes are blasting out of the speakers.

Lindner slips off his stool, pushes it away and dangles himself over the bar so that we can all see him, and waves his index finger in the air.

'None of that would have happened if Bremen had more police, that's a total failure by the senate.'

He actually looks as though he believes what he's saying.

'Bremen doesn't need more police,' says Rocktäschel, showing the barman that we'd like another four vodkas, please. 'Bremen needs Batman.'

My telephone rings, I squint at the display.

Calabretta.

What does he want?

I answer.

We talk for a bit.

By which I mean.

He talks.

I don't say a thing.

Right at the end I say: 'Mm.'

Then we hang up.

I down the vodka, the others look at me.

'Who was that?' asks Stepanovic.

'Calabretta,' I say.

'Any news?'

I move my head to and fro very slowly, it might be a shake, or it might not. Maybe I'm only checking whether I can still move, because it feels as though something very heavy has been pumped into my body.

'Personal,' I say, and lay my hands on the bar. An anchor would be good right now. Could someone throw me an anchor, please? I've drifted into a strong current.

Stepanovic looks at me.

His eyes ask: what?

'All the guys in Hamburg are heading to the airport,' I say. 'To meet someone.'

'Oh, who's that?'

Yeah, who is that?

I say: 'A friend.'

Stepanovic pushes his vodka aside. 'Shall I drive you to Hamburg?'

'No.' My knees start trembling, I can't do anything about it. 'I'll go home tomorrow morning. Right now, I'd rather have another drink.'

STICKS LIKE HELL, BLOOD DOES, BUT SO DOES THE WOMAN

Would you look at her.

Hanging round here, still with that face on.

If the wind changes, she'll be stuck that way.

OK, she can't sleep since the guy next door stopped fucking her and then moved out. To a nice place. Right on the edge of town – for security reasons, presumably. Although she really doesn't seem like the kind of person you have to leave town over. Can't even get up off her arse long enough to actually get on an ex's nerves.

And, yes, she has an alcohol problem, I'm pretty sure of that, although of course she'd never admit it.

But does that mean you have to keep walking into my door frame, stumble over my floorboards, sit in my corners and stare at my walls? Do you have to walk around with a face like someone's forced your heart up against a circular saw? And could you PLEASE at least comb your hair now and then?

Now she's calling the office. Calling in sick for the rest of the day. She's not sick. She's done in. Liar. And it doesn't even bother her when she lies.

Lugging her coffee cup around the place like she doesn't know what to do with it. And then the coffee cup will just end up sitting about somewhere, will it? What's so hard about taking coffee cups with you when you slink from one room to the next? I don't like everything always being left sitting about somewhere. Cold coffee.

Disgusting. She might just as well rub it straight into her hair instead of drinking it: at least then there'd be something going on on her head, even if there's nothing but that gigantic void inside it.

And all the fag ends. The way the nicotine assaults me from every side.

Makes me want to puke.

It's the little things that show you when something's going wrong in a relationship.

The way she showers, for example: that annoys me. The way she dries herself, and always forgets her back, and then her T-shirt always kind of sticks to her from behind. And her hair – she generally forgets to dry her hair and it drips all down her back and onto her T-shirt too.

Someone or other gave her some make-up in the last year. But she doesn't use it. Just don't think about the people who have to look at you every day, huh? Or what?

I'm so sick of her, I'm always thrilled when she's gone out again.

I run off, my hair's still wet and maybe I ought to comb it again, but never mind, you can't think of everything, I'm pleased enough when I can stand up straight. The early summer is yelling at me, the sky is a fierce blue, blasting down at me, the colour takes the direct route through my eyes and goes deep inside; the light is clear and seems to have something brand new in mind, unlike me; I'm just trying to bear the standard light. The brutal light destabilises me and I find it hard to walk straight. When I'm back on track, I realise that the wind today doesn't smell of the North Sea, it smells of the Mediterranean.

I watch her go and I see her stagger.

Watch out, girl; get a grip, Jackie Sparrow, or you'll stumble into somewhere again. But you're used to stumbling, aren't you? So just run along and take a running jump, I'm better off when you're out anyway.

Towards the end of the afternoon, after a half-marathon through Hamburg, which hasn't calmed me a jot, I can't stand it anymore and I call Calabretta.

'OK,' I say, 'where is he?'

'Do you know the apartments at the Police Museum?'

'The old barracks?'

'Mm,' says Calabretta. 'We've lodged him there for the moment. It all had to happen pretty fast, there was information that he wasn't safe in Turkey anymore, as a former German policeman.'

'What about his hotel in Istanbul?'

'I didn't ask.'

'How is he?'

'Dunno. He's grown his hair.'

'He's not the long-hair type.'

'Exactly.'

I light a cigarette and walk a couple of steps without saying anything.

'Apartment five,' Calabretta says eventually, 'the first building you come to.'

'Thanks.'

'*Da nich für*, Chas, don't mention it.'

Did he just call me Chas?

So it's like that now, is it, Vito? I think, and don't know if I'm happy about that, but then a warm wave flows down my back, maybe it's gratitude. That Calabretta's around, even if there are a few deep scratches in his polish now, or maybe even because of that.

I run on through the city, can't decide where I should get into a taxi, and the city acts like it's OK with that, as if it were all right for me just to run around in it without exactly knowing where I'm going, but sometimes I don't trust it. Weird, when we've known each other for so long. Every so often, I almost expect a monster to jump out at me suddenly from between the cars and bite my head off, or someone to block my way and ask me what exactly, if you please, are you for? And then I'll be spat at, jeered at.

Yes, sometimes I have this thing with the city.

I wonder where this feeling comes from.

Sometimes I suspect that my flat is having a go at me behind my back, or something. That I'm not really safe there anymore, that the hole where the flat next door should be is in league with my flat, that that's why I can't sleep there anymore, but of course it's stupid of me to think like that.

The city carries me further north, despite all the monsters, questioners, spitters, they're all in my wake, and then, oh, here we go, at some point I find myself standing outside Bülent Inceman's door.

Apartment number five.

Good morning, I think. What do you say in a case like this?

I knock, and the knock pretends to have guts behind it but, in reality, it's pretty feeble.

The door opens, he looks me over, down to the ground, and he says: 'I wondered when you'd come.'

His hair really is down below his shoulders, black, glossy, smooth, it's like Calabretta said. It's really weird to see him like this, but it's weird in general, and I think: Apache.

And then I fling my arms around his neck, the way I normally never fling my arms around people's necks, and we just stand like that forever and breathe something big and grey away.

Where his right arm used to be, there's only a shoulder.

I stroke the empty sleeve of his T-shirt.

'Maybe we ought to arrange a prothesis for you,' I say, and he says: 'Maybe.'

He takes my hand. 'Come in.'

A bed, a sofa, a table with two chairs, an open holdall in the corner. On the windowsill, an arsenal of medication. Tablets, drops, every form of morphine you could want.

'Does it hurt?' I ask.

'No idea. I don't think about it.'

I don't think about it either, but there are pictures in my head that have never gone away. The evening a couple of years ago – before Stepanovic, before Klatsche – when we were all sitting in a pizzeria, and then the motorbike came. I heard it coming. Since then, the sound of certain motorbikes has sent shivers down my spine.

Then the Molotov cocktails flew like bombs.

Fire, smoke, screams, I had blood on my face, we all did, but Inceman had the most blood everywhere and his arm was gone, and then he was sitting on the plane to Istanbul and he took quite a few things with him, except the blood, which he left behind. It sticks like hell to everyone who was there that evening.

He sits on one of the two chairs and looks at me. He still wears those tight clothes, even if they're not suits anymore, but just jeans and a T-shirt. He's still tall and angular, and his shoulders look as broad as they ever did, but he only has the one arm available for the chasm that he carries around with him. How heavy it must be, heavy as concrete; and hard, hard as nails.

We look at each other for a while, I lay a hand on the table, he lays his beside it.

'This isn't working,' I say and stand up again.

Just sitting opposite each other and looking at each other like this is enough to make your teeth itch.

'Come on,' I say, and now I take his hand, call us a taxi and we head to St Pauli together.

On the car radio they say that cars were set on fire in southern European cities this lunchtime. In Seville, in Marseille, in Genoa, in Bari, in Thessaloniki. The late-afternoon light wraps itself around our three-and-a-half shoulders like a not overly warm blanket.

EVERYTHING THAT'S BEEN LOST IN THE LAST FEW YEARS

We get out at Heiligengeistfeld and walk down to the water. The wind picks up. We walk close to each other but without touching. That's close enough already, I'm finding it pretty strange as it is.

We turn right at the piers, towards the evening sun.

Inceman walks along the quay wall, I walk on the right of him, perhaps I'm walking there to replace something. He keeps his head down and stares at his feet, I try not to look too much in his direction.

He stops just outside Brücke 10, raises his head and shuts his eyes. A gull is flying right above us. It stops, hangs in the air, then plummets into the Elbe. It pulls something out. A warship is in dock at Blohm & Voss: it really is in urgent need of repair if anyone wants to win anything with it.

'What's the light like in Istanbul?' I ask.

'Warm and colourful,' he says. 'It has a few extra tones. But it isn't as bright as here.'

'And what's happening with your hotel now?'

He opens his eyes again and looks at the water.

'I didn't even lock up. Maybe then they won't bother kicking the door down.'

'Why did everything have to happen so quickly?'

'They arrested my business partner two nights ago, no idea

why, he never did anything, never even said anything, I thought we weren't even on their radar. Why should we be? Almost all our clients were German tourists and, even then, I kept my mouth shut like a good boy, as a German citizen and former cop.'

'Shall we grab a beer?'

He nods, I get two bottles of Astra from the bar at Brücke 10 and open them with my lighter.

'They probably arrested him to intimidate me,' he says. 'Suddenly it didn't suit somebody to have me there. I got a lawyer for him, packed my stuff and hopped on the next plane.'

'Can we do anything for your friend?' I ask, handing him his beer.

'I'm paying the lawyer.'

We sit back to back on a harbour bollard on the quay wall, the waves swim past below, some of them are topped by a gull, sometimes there's a bit of rubbish there too, or just muck. The ferry from the Sandtorkai to Finkenwerder goes past. We drink.

'How are you?' he asks.

I shrug my shoulders. 'I'm tired. I can't sleep anymore.'

'Join the club.'

'But you've got all those tablets,' I say.

'What they give isn't sleep,' he says. 'It's anaesthesia. I'd give my right arm to do without them, if I still had one left.'

His back twitches a little, and as he's not the kind of guy who cries, I guess he's laughing. At his own stupid joke.

I swig the beer and watch the ferries as they pass, it seems like they're smiling. The brave, encouraging type of smile that only little ships on big bodies of water can rustle up.

'Thanks for coming and not leaving me alone in that stupid apartment,' he says. 'I wasn't totally sure that you would.'

'Well,' I say, and turn towards him so that I'm sitting kind of next to him and kind of behind him. 'I had to think it over a bit.'

He turns and looks at me. 'Whether you're in the mood for a cripple.'

'That kind of thing.'

'It's still nuts,' he says, 'your way with people.'

I find myself grinning, his stupid laugh just now released something.

'If I punch you, will you feel it? With all the morphine and that?'

'No,' he says. 'Punch away.'

I don't punch him. I hook my right arm under his left, then I rest my head on his shoulder as if it were nothing, and I suddenly feel very young, and then we sit there stuck to each other and drink up our beer, but we're careful not to do it too quickly.

At some point I stand up and get us two more beers.

I can't sit back down with him.

First, I have to get used to him being here again. I look at him and it's as if a wall of reinforced concrete has started to crumble, I can hear something trickling.

'Come on,' I say, 'let's walk some more.'

We start by climbing the harbour steps, and then go to the Blue Night. He's still got that loose, cat-like walk, but his injury wraps itself tightly around us, around the things we say, around our every movement. Here's everything that's got lost in the last few years.

I stop, he looks at me.

'We'll make it through together,' I say.

We're the quintessential buddy movie.

AS IF IT HAD EVER BEEN POSSIBLE TO EXPLAIN ANYTHING

There are a few last rays of sunlight lying around in the pub. Carla hangs her coat over a chair. Rocco lights candles. Schulle, Brückner and Faller have set themselves on stools like bar ornaments, each with a bottle of beer and a cigarette in hand. Last night's glasses are standing on the scuffed wooden bar, lemon rind still shimmering in some of them, while others only hold puddles of whatever, the main point being that people's minds went south with it, at least for a couple of hours.

All in all, the scenery looks as though they've dropped one of those Dutch Old Masters here, one of the ones with all those dirty colours everywhere, and that lived stuff.

Faller's, Schulle's and Brückner's expressions spill cautious affection when they see us come in. Carla stretches and tilts her head, it's the pose she always adopts when something happens that confuses her. Rocco's stopped lighting the candles and kneads a bit of wax between his fingers.

Inceman strokes back his Apache hair.

'Our man in Istanbul,' says Faller and spreads out his arms. 'Nice to see you again.'

Inceman goes over to him and actually accepts the embrace, and then from Schulle and Brückner too, but they do something more like clapping him on the back; he hesitates by Carla for a moment, and then that doesn't matter either.

Everyone gulps a bit; everyone pushes away the stuff that needs pushing away just then.

I order beer for us and a round of shots. Inceman walks over to the jukebox, shoves his left hand in his trouser pocket and chucks in a few euros.

Ah.

Tindersticks.

Rented Rooms, we go fuck in the bathroom.

It's almost a bit like old times.

Except the arm's missing.

And Klatsche's missing, but sorry, I don't want to talk about that.

But then when I join him at the jukebox with our beers in my hand, the Apache asks where my boyfriend is.

I look at my beer bottle, then I look at him, then I shrug my shoulders, didn't I just say that I don't want to talk about it, for fuck's sake, and then I say it anyway: 'Bringing up a child.'

That's quite enough now.

'Ah, OK,' says Inceman and he understands that it's enough, that we'd maybe better change the subject. 'And where's my friend? Where's the guy who was so mad keen to pick me up from the airport yesterday?'

'Calabretta?'

'Yeah, that's the guy. Starts by organising a massive hello and then doesn't reappear.'

'Uh, complicated,' I say and lean against the jukebox and, in a way, I'm leaning against the music. 'I'll explain another time.'

As if I'd ever been able to explain anything.

Things aren't all that good between Calabretta and Rocco right now. Because things were pretty good between Calabretta and Carla for a while and sometimes they presumably still are, depending on how the season's going, depending on the weather, depending on their general state of health, hunger, thirst, stuff like that, but none of us knows exactly, even the three of them don't really know what's going on, I don't think. At any rate, Rocco would rather not know anything about it, so Vito Calabretta's barred from here at the moment, and that's why I can't say too much about it now either.

'Let's have a schnapps,' I say, and Inceman nods. Being with him is like being with one of those exchange students who used to come to visit. Come on, I'll show you my world and now we'll do this and then we'll do that, and the exchange student is too uncertain and too new to want anything for themselves, and then they just join in with everything and it's OK. Except that there's nobody new here, because all of us have had some part of us fucked up at some point.

We join the others at the bar and drink. The alcohol, the music, the faces, the scars, it all goes straight to my belly. I'd like to have somewhere to lean on and I wish Stepanovic were here, but he's probably scrambling about somewhere in a personal capacity, so that he can leave another part of himself lying around in a strange bed until the sun finally crawls over the horizon.

When I notice Carla standing beside me, I just lean against her and let air out of my lungs.

'Hard to breathe here, hm?' she says.

'No use anyway,' I say.

Faller lays a hand on Inceman's right half-shoulder and he doesn't flinch, which I find astonishing. I'd have flinched.

'I've had a great idea for what we can do with you, by the way!'

Like an exchange student? I think, and I can't quite get back on board again, exhaled too much oxygen, perhaps.

'Doing something would be good,' says Inceman. 'But I'm more of the unfit-for-duty type, you know.'

'Unfit for duty is absolutely perfect for my idea,' says Faller.

Everyone very quietly puts down their beer and pricks up their ears, even Rocco, who, as a former small-time criminal, isn't usually all that interested in the perfect police idea, but the words 'unfit for duty' probably ring some bell with everyone.

'I've been working at the Police Museum lately,' says Faller. 'I've been showing school classes around the exhibition for a month or so.'

Everyone relaxes again. Police Museum, oh right, super-boring.

'You want me to do something with school classes?'

Inceman looks at Faller like he's pressed a glass of sour milk on him. The ex-hard-core cop, ex-drugs squad, ex-murder squad, famous victim of an attack by the Albanian mafia, now a brand-new kiddies' entertainer.

'I don't want you to do anything,' says Faller and looks back, mildly piqued. 'But we're always looking for experienced staff who can support us.'

Experienced staff, aha. Maybe I should sign up there too. Then maybe I could show the kids what happens if you get too much experience.

'In the press office, for example,' says Faller, putting his beer away. 'There's been no one there for over a year. And we just can't find anyone who wants to do it. Couldn't that be something for you?'

'I don't know,' says Inceman.

I don't know either. A desk Inceman.

'Think about it, at least,' says Faller, pushing back his hat. 'All the guys there are unfit for duty. It's a really nice atmosphere.'

SMOKE GETS IN YOUR EYES

RILEY
I've got pub smoke in my eyes, or whatever kind of smoke it is.
Maybe it didn't even come from the pub, maybe it's come from
my head, maybe it's come from my heart. You can't see through
it. I can't handle it, being in the middle of all this, I just can't
handle it. Sitting next to it is OK.

Maybe I can make something out of it.

INCEMAN
The flight response has vanished. Everything is pretty bearable.
And then her hard beauty. Her molten core. If that erupts, then
it's worth it. Seventeen men on the dead man's chest, and the
chest is full of rum.

CARLA
Nobody sees anything. Nobody asks. Nobody dares. I'm on
my own side. I am where I am and where I want to be.
Sometimes here, sometimes there, sometimes gone. I'm not in
charge. I go out and go in and come again. I pick stuff up and
drop it again. Climb, dive, sail on the wind. There's something
gull-like about it.

ROCCO
They pity me. They have no idea. We're lions. A pack is helpful but you can manage without. My lioness and me, we are the way we are. I let her go, she always comes back. And I'm running the show here. It's my show now. I just mustn't ever forget the candles. I light them, I blow them out.

CALABRETTA
Oh, you know. I'm busy. If not, I'm running around, like I've always done. Something will turn up.

BRÜCKNER AND SCHULLE
Guys! It was years ago! It was the middle of the night, in the Sorgenbrecher, they were dancing on the bar, they both had red curls down to their arses, and they both had a beer brand tattooed on their calves. And we were standing in front of the bar with beer bottles in our hands and we acted like we were dancing with them, but in truth we were just drunk on those twin women. Never been in love since. It's a crock of shit after all.

ROCKTÄSCHEL
There's a lump of tar, it hasn't moved for years, hasn't grown, sometimes I thought the lump wasn't even there anymore. But now it's getting bigger, firmer, darker, and it's eating its way out from the inside. Fuck the fuck off, you fucking lump.

FALLER
Everything's mixed up and I very often don't understand it anymore, but then I smoke a Roth-Händle and doff my hat to the world and then I put the hat on again and then I try to stay.

STEPANOVIC
It'll be all right again. One day it will be. Believe firmly in that and keep making loads of bad jokes and eventually I'll tell her, and then, yes then: it'll be all right.

LINDNER
What's actually going on here?

NOURI

Sometimes he lost things on purpose, just for the feeling that flooded his belly when he found them again. He left a huge range of things lying around all over the place. Gym bags, books, toys, jack knives. He'd always named things in advance, written *Nouri S.* on them with a thick, black felt-tip so that there was a greater chance of someone taking the stuff to the lost-property office. The lost-property office was only a few doors down from his primary school, every day after school he popped by to see if he'd find anything again.

'You're a real expert at losing things,' the woman behind the glass pane sometimes said to him, and he'd think: Nah. The other way round. I'm an expert at finding things.

It was just too nice.

He'd never quite understood exactly what was so good about it, about letting go of something and then seeing if and when it came back, but there was a lightness in it that was unfamiliar to him. It was fun.

At home, nothing was ever fun or light or easy. They said even his birth had been hard. He hadn't wanted to come out, his father had said once, not until his father had beaten his mother on the back with his stick; then it had worked. That was the first and last time that Nouri had asked about 26th February 1990, the day of his birth. Because everything was stupid enough already. His mother might not hit anyone with a stick, but she had her wooden spoon. She hit out with that whenever the children did or said anything she thought was wrong, and she thought almost everything that Nouri, his three older brothers and four sisters said and did was wrong. At mealtimes they were all very quiet, because at mealtimes their father was there too and he had his stick. Mother was going to have another baby soon, her belly was already very fat. Then there'd be nine of them. Nouri hoped that his father wouldn't have to use his stick again to make the baby come out. His mother had just turned twenty-nine but Nouri sometimes thought she was already much older, at least sixty or something. Maybe because she never laughed.

But why should she, Nouri thought when he thought about what everything was, and why everything was the way it was, and then slipped into a dark hole that opened up within him, meaning that he slipped inside himself, and then it was so dark in there that he was afraid. That was why he preferred not to think about it too often.

In the evenings, when he lay in bed, he imagined what it would be like if everything were different. If he were called Müller or Schmidt or something else German, like the other children at his school. If he had a name that didn't always make everyone get that funny look on their faces as soon as they heard it.

They looked at him as if he were dangerous.

But he didn't think he was dangerous at all. He didn't even fetch his brothers if there was trouble over anything. His brother Mahmud, who was in year four, OK, *he* did that. He told Ali and Hamsa right away if anyone at school annoyed him. Then Ali and Hamsa came by the playground the next day, and then the kid who'd had trouble with Mahmud would have to look out in case he ended up in the corner behind the sports hall that was so hard to see into and where there was never a teacher around just because the teachers were needed somewhere else.

Nouri didn't want his big brothers to beat anyone up for him. He didn't even tell Mahmud. He just walked away if there was trouble with anyone over anything.

He never had trouble with the teachers, Nouri did well at school. He could read very fluently for year two, writing wasn't a problem either, maths was his favourite subject. He liked those complicated puzzle problems best of all, the ones where you had to spend ages thinking around them till you found the answer. Nouri always found it, and usually faster than anyone else.

Sometimes he even thought up his own puzzle problems late in the evening when he was lying in his bed at home and couldn't get to sleep, firstly because he was thinking about his life and his family, and secondly because these women were talking so loudly outside, under his window, about money and foreign languages.

'French for fifty, shit, man, that just screws up the prices!'

They called out all kinds of other stuff through the night, but Nouri didn't understand what it was about.

One morning, his sister Leyli had asked his mother what the women in the street were always talking about, but there was no answer, there was only the wooden spoon. Leyli had been three then.

Nouri had decided that one day he'd ask the other children on the street exactly what the thing was, exactly who these women were, and why they always stood around on the streets at night. And the other thing he urgently needed to ask the others was whether or not they were his friends. When they spent the afternoons running around the neighbourhood together, he thought: yes. When he wasn't invited to their birthdays, or when the mothers banned their sons from playing with him, when he stood outside the doors and those doors were shut again, softly but firmly, without letting him come through, then he thought: actually, probably not.

He suspected that it was to do with his father, with his brothers, with his uncles, with his cousins. With all that stuff that wasn't like other families. German families where the fathers didn't go to work were poor. His father didn't go to work either, he always said that he'd actually like to work, but he wasn't allowed to, and so he didn't have any work, but they had two cars all the same, and lived in a house that belonged to them. Where did the money for the cars and the house come from? Tim's mother had asked him that once, she'd really grilled him. Nouri had looked at her and not known what he was meant to answer, he hadn't even really understood the question.

He couldn't ask about the business with the money at home, because of the business with the stick.

When he was running around the place with the others, who he hoped were his friends, when they laughed together and messed around and collected stuff, he didn't think about the questions he had for his parents. Those were the moments when he didn't wonder about all that. When he wasn't Nouri Saroukhan but Nurra. That was his gang name, the same way that Tim was called Timma in the gang, Julius was Julla and Fabrizio was Fabba. They spent hours just rolling around the neighbourhood, they rolled around and told each other who they'd like to be, which superheroes, which baddies, which Werder players, stuff like that. It would have been enough for Nouri if he could always just have been Nurra.

When the others weren't out, because they weren't allowed out with him, or they'd been invited to a birthday party, he was neither Nurra nor Nouri. When he was alone, he was nobody at all.

Then, nobody at all generally walked down to the Weser, took the Sielwall ferry over to the Stadtwerder peninsula, where he hid in the woods.

Then, among the trees and branches and leaves, he could forget that he was nobody at all.

ALIZA

Really, there was trouble every day. She was just the in-trouble type.

'This girl means trouble,' a teacher had recently said, in English, in front of the whole class. He'd grinned as he said it and he'd meant it appreciatively, because in his world it was right and proper for a girl to live wild and free and not to be told.

In Aliza's world, that wasn't good. There, a rebellious girl was the worst thing that could ever happen, especially to the rebellious girl. Aliza was beaten every day; she didn't know anything else. And the more she got beaten, the more rebellious she became.

So there were more beatings.

When the beatings came, she closed her eyes and closed off her heart and dreamt herself away. At some point she'd learnt not to feel the beatings anymore.

She was the youngest of eight children, she had five older sisters and two older brothers. Dinara, the eldest sister, had vanished at the beginning of the year, the others said she'd got married but Aliza didn't believe them because there hadn't been a party, just that night when there'd been a cousin that Aliza had never seen before. He'd taken Dinara with him into the little room at the end of the hall. Dinara hadn't screamed or anything, but Aliza had heard her whimpering and she knew that the cousin was hurting her. When he'd finished, he'd given Mohamed, the oldest brother, an envelope and then he'd taken Dinara away with him.

Aliza hadn't understood any of what had happened to Dinara, but on that night she'd realised that it would also be part of her future at some point to vanish first into that room and then out of the house.

The house was on the west bank of the Weser, in Buntentor: the place was named after a colourful gate, and outside the house was a colourful street where lots of different people wandered around every day and every evening, there were colourful shops, a very colourful kiosk where you could buy even more colourful ice cream, and there was Bruno, who had the old workshop on Hoffmannstrasse. Going to see Bruno wasn't allowed – because Aliza and her sisters basically weren't allowed to do anything – but Aliza went to Bruno's workshop every day and knocked on the back door. Bruno was a small man with a bald head. Aliza didn't quite know whether he was old or, maybe, not that old at all really, but just wrinkled and kind of dried-up, but she didn't actually care. He was small, he wore a brown leather apron, there were lots of tools hanging from his belt, and he was friendly to children. You could always knock and then you'd get given something that you could work on; more often than not, you were allowed to carve something.

Whenever Bruno pressed the woodcarving knife into Aliza's hand and said, 'You can make what you like,' and whenever she then carved something out of a piece of wood, an animal, a flower, a ship, then with every shaving that fell to the floor, her heart, hardened by beatings, grew a little softer again.

NOURI AND ALIZA, OR:
NO, THANK YOU, NO EEL SANDWICH FOR US PLEASE

It was the summer that Ailton came to Werder Bremen. Nouri played football with the other boys from the neighbourhood. On the Stadtwerder, the semi-wild peninsula in the Weser. He played for the under-tens. They trained twice a week. Hardly anyone took the Sielwall ferry straight back after training, almost everyone went swimming, to snatch another hour's freedom before they had to be sitting at the table at home with washed hands.

Lots of kids from the west of Bremen swam in the Werdersee too, from the Buntentor area where there was a pedestrian bridge onto the island, jump on your bike, zip across, zap to the beach.

Nouri wasn't a particularly good swimmer. He more sort of splashed around, watched the others and studied the water.

One day, there was this dead animal. Floating towards him on the surface of the water. At first, he thought the animal was a stick, was about to touch it, when he noticed that it wasn't wood but a kind of slimy snake or maybe even a fish.

'Ugh, eels are so gross,' said someone standing right behind him.

He turned around.

A girl.

Black hair, dark skin. Nouri thought the girl looked a bit like him, even if it's always hard to tell that yourself, but there was something there.

He waded a little towards the bank, away from the dead eel, the girl came with him. She looked at him as if she were looking right inside him and could see everything.

'Not as gross as all that.'

He acted as though he'd known all along that it had been an eel in the water there, and he was slightly embarrassed that a little girl had had to come along and explain that to him.

She carried on giving him a crystal-clear stare. 'I don't mean the animal. I mean to eat. Have you ever had eel?'

He shook his head, but he sensed that he didn't feel much like eating a fish that looked like a slimy snake. He sat on the bank in the shallow water, she sat beside him. The sun crashed down on their wet hair.

'Bruno sometimes makes himself eel sandwiches, ew, so bad, I really can't stand them.'

'Who's Bruno?' he asked.

'A handyman,' she said. 'And who are you?'

'Nouri.'

He looked at her and wrapped his arms around his knees. She really looked quite a lot like him, he thought.

'How about you?'

'Aliza. I live over there.'

She pointed to the Buntentor neighbourhood. She turned over and lay with her belly in the sand.

'I live over there,' said Nouri, tilting his head back and to the left.

Aliza drew circles in a puddle with her fingers.

'Do you like sweets?'

'Of course,' said Nouri. 'Have you got some?'

She nodded and grinned at him, and now he could catch a glimpse of everything she was. She was like him only a great deal braver.

Aliza stood up, went to her rucksack and came back with a really impressive bag of sweets.

They sat in the sand till the shadows grew longer. After half an hour, they'd eaten all the sweets, but their heads were too full to just go.

When Aliza got home, there was a beating.

She'd taken the money for the sweets from her mother, she'd been outside again and, worse still, she'd been swimming, she was dirty and stupid and utterly good for nothing, it was about time she got that.

When Nori got home, the darkness in the hallway punched him in the face.

The very next afternoon, he took the ferry over to the Stadtwerder again and headed for the beach on the other side of the island. He ran as fast as he could. Aliza was just throwing her bike down in the sand when he came running through the bushes. She held up a bag of sweets.

That was how things were from then on, as often as possible.

They met almost every day on their island.

On the beach.

Between the allotments.

Behind the tennis courts.

At the Skipper Inn at the Sailing Club.

Under the elder bushes.

In the Kids' Wilderness.

When they said goodbye, Aliza always walked with Nouri to the ferry, then she rode her bike right back across the island to go home and collect her beating.

Nouri watched her from the ferry and thought, every time, that she was one of the craziest girls he knew, but also the best by a long way.

Over the years, while they kept meeting, while they were growing older, things happened.

Nouri went to the grammar school, the only one in his family who ever had. None of his brothers, none of his cousins, nobody had been to the grammar school. Why should they? You made money in the family business, not at uni. But because Nouri's teachers kept saying that he really ought to go to university, his father eventually said: fine, he can go to university and be a lawyer and we'll just have him for that.

His brothers all started stealing at the age of twelve; by fifteen, at the latest, they were selling drugs; by eighteen, they were selling stolen cars too, and you just picked up how to handle guns and the police along the way.

Nouri wasn't allowed to do any of that, and he didn't want to either.

When he told Aliza, at the end of year four, that he was going to the grammar school and that he was meant to be going to uni later too, she whacked him one and ran away and didn't appear on the beach for three days.

Nouri guessed why she'd done it. She was at least as clever as him, if not cleverer, maybe. But she was a girl. In their families, girls didn't go to school any longer than they absolutely had to. Nouri had never heard of a girl in their families going to the grammar school. That just wasn't for girls.

In year five, Aliza was sent to the local high school in her neighbourhood. Her rage often boiled over so fiercely that she collected even more beatings from then on, although that wasn't really possible because there was nowhere left to hit, everywhere was already full.

She'd wanted to be an astronaut.

Now she talked for the first time about just running away. She told him about her sisters who'd disappeared, two of them by then: Dinara and Leila. She told Nouri what always happened when her sisters had to go with their cousins, first into the little room and then away, and she said: 'I swear, they'll never get me in there, in that crappy room. I'll be gone by then.'

Nouri didn't really believe Aliza, because how could that work, just running away? They'd catch you, they'd bring you back, but he did still believe her a little bit. The way she was.

He was proud of her because she said things like that. He didn't even dare think about that kind of thing. He wasn't the type to do crazy stuff.

But things were different for him, he knew that. He was doing well. He didn't get a beating every day. He'd go to university. He was a boy. And his father was powerful, his family was rich. At some point, Nouri guessed where the wealth came from, but even then, he didn't really dare to think about it. Until one afternoon when Aliza pulled the veil away. They were strolling through the wilderness, at the pool, it was summer but not the weather for swimming, it was drizzling.

Aliza was ranting.

The evening before, her father hadn't been there, and her mother hadn't felt like giving Aliza her beating. She'd just called a couple of cousins and asked who had time to come and dish out a few slaps. The one who'd taken Dinara had time and so had his brother, so they came over so that Aliza would get her beating.

Her mother always hit her so that it didn't show that much,

she never hit her in the face. The cousins didn't care about her face. Aliza had a black eye and a split lip.

'Those criminal arseholes. I wish they were all finally in jail.'

She kicked aside a few branches; the leaves rustled under their feet.

'I don't understand why they're not in jail, all the men in our families ought to be in jail, I hate them.'

She swore and kept kicking branches and swore, and at some point, she just sat down on the wet ground and cried. She looked at Nouri, the tears were running down her cheeks as if someone had been holding a river prisoner behind her eyes, it was the first time Nouri had seen her crying.

'Stupid gangster family,' she said and the tears ran down into her mouth. 'Shitting shit-faced gangster family. They can all kiss my arse. And when I'm grown up, I'll grass them up, as often as I can, I'll go to the cops every pissing day and grass those wankers up.'

Nouri knew that she was right about everything, but he couldn't get a single word out.

'And your shitting dad,' she said, 'he's the shitting boss of this whole crappy pile of shit. And my shitting dad isn't even a shitting boss, he's just a stupid little idiot of a gangster, and that makes him a pissed-off idiot of a gangster, and that's why I keep getting beatings and I'm not allowed to do anything.'

She stood up and glared at him.

'Now would you please say something, just for once!'

Everything you're saying is true, thought Nouri, and he knew he mustn't abandon her now, he had to say something about it so that her eye wouldn't hurt so much, her lip, her life. He thought. And then he thought of something.

'They all act,' he said, 'like they're the greatest. Like they're not scared of anything and they're so dangerous and chiefs and important and strong and that. But they only do that because they know that they're really small and actually aren't allowed to do anything and none of them have proper jobs. They're really scared. You're the only one of all of us who's not afraid of anything.'

Aliza sniffed and gave a slightly wonky grin and said: 'Apart from me and you, they're all stupid scaredy-arses.'

Nouri shrugged his shoulders and nodded and grinned, and they stood there like that for a bit and nodded and giggled and said, yes, yes they are.

As Nouri and Aliza grew older, Aliza spoke more and more often about what it would be like to just run away. And at some point, Nouri started talking about it too.

'Mexico,' he said once, 'we'll go to Mexico. Nobody will find us there and there's always a warm wind blowing.'

Aliza looked at him, a thousand furrows in her brow.

'It's called Mehico.'

'OK, Mehico. We'll go there then. Or at least to Hamburg.'

Aliza had said a couple of times that one day she'd just run away to Hamburg, the closest big city, where she'd go underground and sod the lot of them.

'We're not going anywhere,' she said, speaking very seriously. 'I'm going.'

'I want to go with you,' said Nouri.

'If we run away together, it'll be too obvious. If we go, each of us goes alone.'

There were moments between them when Nouri had the feeling that Aliza would eat him alive if it were necessary to get to her goal. Because Aliza always did what she thought was necessary.

In her opinion, it was not necessary for more sisters to disappear.

First Zahara.

Then Samira.

The sisters didn't defend themselves. They whimpered and were gone.

Sometimes Aliza thought that maybe that was all they deserved. She'd damn well defend herself.

Then came the night when Melika disappeared.

It was summer. Aliza was fourteen, Nouri had turned fifteen in the spring. They'd been out for a long time, and on their island, they'd swum and sat in the sand, then they'd hung around on Buntentorsteinweg for a while, at a safe distance from Aliza's flat. Nouri had bought ice cream, they'd sat on the pavement. At around ten, Nouri said: 'I'd better take you home or you'll get another...'

'It's OK,' said Aliza.

They heard the shouting as they came round the corner. Banging and slamming. A woman screamed, a man screamed back.

'Melika,' said Aliza. 'That's Melika.'

She froze and grabbed Nouri's hand. A tall, fat man came out of the building Aliza's family lived in, he had his hood up and was dragging a thin, young woman behind him. By her hair. The young woman screamed and wept but nobody helped her. The people preferred to look away. Her skirt was torn, there was blood running down the insides of her legs. The man dragged her to a car parked on the other side of the road, she screamed louder, he slammed his fist into her face.

Aliza pulled away from Nouri and ran towards her sister, who was now perfectly still. She lay on the ground and was no longer moving.

Even before Aliza reached her, the tall, fat man caught her a long right hook to the chin, Aliza was small and light, she flew a good six feet and landed in the road.

Nouri didn't know what to do. He really oughtn't to be there, if they found out that Aliza was meeting a boy, they'd lock her up forever or beat her to death on the spot, and maybe they would anyway now. The man gave Aliza a kick in the belly and when she doubled up, he gave her a kick in the back too, then he hauled Melika into the car by her arm, and then he turned around and now, for the first time, he looked towards where Nouri was standing behind a tree. The man's hood slipped, revealing his face.

The tall, fat man was Nouri's eldest brother, Ali. Ali got into the car and drove away.

Nouri didn't dare go over, but he didn't dare leave either, so he carried on standing behind his tree and waited till they came out and took Aliza in.

THE FIRST AVAILABLE TRAIN

Outside Bruno's workshop. The poppies in flower in the cracks in the asphalt. Yellow and orange. Not the sort that flower everywhere.

They were special poppies.

Strange poppies.

Favourite poppies.

She looked through the window again, saw Bruno sitting at his workbench. Now he was definitely old.

'Do what you want,' he'd always said to her, and she thought: OK, I will.

She laid her hand on the window, Bruno turned around and smiled at her, she took her hand away again and smiled back, and then she went.

Down Buntentorsteinweg to Leibnizplatz.

Past the school.

She found it hard to walk because of the kicks to her belly and back the evening before, and also because of Nouri.

But she couldn't take him with her, she could only take herself, that was hard enough as it was.

She got on the bus on the bridge.

She got off at the station and then she got on again, this time on the first available train.

And then she was finally gone.

RIDE ON

She didn't come to the island anymore. For the first few days, Nouri thought Ali might have hospitalised her, so he trudged round all the hospitals, but she wasn't there. He kept on waiting on the beach, but she stayed away. He hoped she'd come back in the autumn. When winter came, he realised that Aliza had gone.

She'd actually done it, and she'd done it the way she'd said she would. No telling him where she was going, no goodbyes, no risks.

'So no one can beat where I am out of you.'

Nouri went to school, in the afternoons he went to kung fu, so that there'd be no way anyone could beat anything out of him, he rode his bike through the tunnel to training and, every time, he thought he ought to ride on to the station and just see what happened, what train would come along, what kind of life, and everything.

At night, in his dreams, when he was at risk of drowning, a dead eel came past and rescued him.

HELLO, THIS IS YOUR HOLE OF AN OFFICE SPEAKING

I'm sitting in my office at the public prosecution service, I've got a few things to take care of and I need to bring the Attorney General up to speed. But they could save themselves the expense, really.

Of my so-called office, I mean.

It's still that hellhole between two walls without a proper window. The phone line's died now too, and I haven't been in court for ages. I'm in this permanent state of limbo: sometimes I'm in charge of something, sometimes it's better if I'm not, and I only ever work as an investigating prosecutor. I'm assigned when nobody else has time, or when my boss thinks: this thing that's happened is enough of a mess for Riley.

That's how it seems.

Either way, I'm only there in the public prosecution service to shoot the legal road clear for the relevant state criminal-investigation office. As a job description, that's perfectly fine by me, of course.

But it doesn't require a hole of an office at the prosecution service.

An office at the police HQ would do. Or, seeing that I generally loathe offices anyway, a small container in the car park for official vehicles. I'd smoke and wave the cars off, and at least I'd have a bit of a view.

Office, what do you say to that?
I say bugger all.

RED HAIR

Over the course of yesterday, when I had to look after Turkey, and Stepanovic was still in Bremen with Baumann, the large, white board that hangs on the wall of the team office filled up. There are now photos between the notes in fat handwriting: of the crime scene, of Nouri Saroukhan's body, a few photos from our corpse's flat, and countless, fuzzy, slightly creased pictures of the harbour at night.

'What are all those harbour photos?' I ask.

'They were all over the place in his flat,' says Anne Stanislawski. She's leaning on the table in the middle of the room and has a pen and a pad in her hand. 'But it didn't look as though someone had just recently spread them around. More like they were part of the decor. If you can really call it decor.'

The pictures from the bedsit look like a somewhat unlovingly assembled page from a furniture catalogue. A bed, a couch, a bar table by the kitchenette, two bar stools, a TV. And on the only continuous wall there are two posters, just pinned up, for which the lousy interior designer would have earnt a slap from the catalogue boss in person. In one of the posters, you can make out Jean-Paul Belmondo. A scene from *The Professional*, I think it's the last moment just before he's shot. The other poster is of a South American cemetery by night: an enormous site with flower-bedecked graves and candles everywhere, the cemetery glows brightly against a background of orange and deep blue, the poster looks like a window into another world.

'Yes,' says Anne Stanislawski, who has noticed my expression, 'and then there were all those harbour photos lying around.'

'Yearning,' I say, and Calabretta, who's sitting with his feet resting on the edge of his desk, says: 'Well, hello.'

'Anything else noticeable in the place?' asks Stepanovic.

The murder squad shake their heads, Schulle and Brückner are engrossed in something on Brückner's computer.

'It's like only pictures live there,' says Anne Stanislawski, tucking her hair behind her ears. 'I've been wondering all morning who that guy really was. And as soon as I get the feeling of having got hold of him for a second, he falls apart in my head again.'

We pool what we know.

Stepanovic talks and writes on the board:

Who are the Mhallami, where do they come from, how do they live here, how do their clan structures work, inwardly and outwardly, who plays what role in the Saroukhan family, and how can we finally get bloody Batman to move to Bremen?

'Nouri Saroukhan must have been cast out by his family while he was still doing his law degree,' says Stepanovic finally. 'Have you found anything that fits with that?'

Calabretta nods, takes his feet off the desk and crosses his legs. 'Up to 2013, Saroukhan was preparing for his exams with a private tutor, like every other law student who gets decent support from home.'

Private tutor. I remember. The memory thinks about sending shivers down my spine. Being a lawyer is reasonably OK, in my opinion, at least it's not particularly painful. But I found the degree shit throughout.

'Tutoring like that costs three hundred euros a month,' says Calabretta, 'plus a good five hundred euros in rent for his digs, excluding bills – it all adds up. So as a student, if you don't get money from your parents or whoever else every month, you're pretty screwed. And Nouri Saroukhan's money clearly ran out suddenly. At the end of twenty-thirteen, he quit the private tutor and signed up for free revision at the uni. That could well have been the time when his family cut off his support.'

'That's usually the first step towards dropping out of a law degree,' I say. 'I only managed because I could live in my dad's flat and didn't have to pay rent. And because he left me a bit.'

A memory crosses my path. I give it the boot.

Calabretta places his feet back on the desk. 'Six months later, he was no longer registered at the university and had got a job at AKTO Insurance.'

'What kind of joint is that?' asks Rocktäschel.

He's standing by the window, holding his flying jacket in his hand as if he's not stopping.

'Common or garden insurance firm in City Nord,' says Calabretta, 'they sell everything from property insurance through to complicated financial services. Saroukhan worked in sales there – as a traditional insurance agent. We spoke to his boss and his colleagues yesterday and the day before. The boss says he was one of his best salesmen. Although I got the impression he hadn't really liked him. But then, I didn't like *him*.'

'Saroukhan must have been earning pretty well, then,' says Stepanovic.

'Here,' says Schulle, raising his hand. 'We're just having a closer look at his bank account. And it does look bloody good. He was making five to six thousand a month, sometimes even more. Financially at least, he did well out of jacking in his degree.'

'And his colleagues?' I ask. 'What do they say about him?'

'The extreme pressure at work didn't seem to bother him,' says Anne Stanislawski. 'At least, his colleagues describe him as having strong nerves, someone who didn't get rattled easily. Apart from that, he seems to have mostly kept out of everything.'

'What do you mean, kept out of?' I ask.

'He didn't join in with all that shit,' says Stanislawski. 'All that macho shit.'

'Flashy cars, flashy parties, flashy-breasted women,' says Calabretta, flashing his eyes. 'Goes with the territory when you work in sales. Sales is the financial services equivalent of motor racing.'

'I was astonished,' says Stanislawski, 'that there wasn't a single woman working in that whole place.'

'Hang on,' says Calabretta, 'there was a secretary on reception.'

'That figures, man, duh.' Anne Stanislawski pulls a face to match the sentence and says: 'I was interested by the only colleague who was kind of friends with Saroukhan. He mentioned that woman.'

'What woman?' asks Stepanovic.

'A girlfriend, possibly,' says Calabretta. 'Nouri Saroukhan doesn't seem to have had much social contact, there were no friends, it was like he had no private life, or at least nothing that he ever told his colleagues about. Just this one woman. There were set evenings when they met and he didn't take any work appointments.'

'The guy thought for ages that the woman didn't really exist,' says Anne Stanislawski, 'that she was only in Nouri's imagination. But then he saw them both down at the harbour one night.'

'Have we got a name for the woman?'

Stepanovic suddenly has very crisp outlines, he's standing up straight, filling the whole room; he looks as though he's picked up a scent.

Anne Stanislawski shakes her head. 'But we've got a pretty good description of her.'

'Red hair?'

'Red hair.'

SUCKING ON SHARDS

Two people, both in their mid-forties, both tall, both long haired. Hers reaches down to her back and is chestnut brown; here and there, the colour's going a bit see-through. His is black and glossy and shoulder length – Apache hair. She's wearing a trench coat, a T-shirt, jeans, ankle boots. He's wearing some kind of jacket instead of the trench coat. She's missing those female accessories, a handbag or a hairstyle or something. He's missing his right arm.

They walk through the streets and take in every bar, and then they sit there and drink and look at each other as if they had something to catch up on but it wasn't available anywhere anymore. Sometimes he holds her hand, sometimes she holds his.

They seem to live in another time. Their time runs more slowly than the time of the others around them, who move quickly, sometimes running here and sometimes there, who dance to the music or kick each other in the ribs. Real time passes them by completely. They're somewhere else entirely, there are only the two of them, and they've got two beers in front of them, and they've got cigarettes in their hands, and sometimes they lay a hand on a cheek, or on a memory.

The neon signs glow their way, hour by hour, into their hearts, their faces look as though they're sucking on shards.

At the end of the night, they stand outside a front door and can't separate, it's going to take the correct time to come by and cut them apart.

The trick is to keep smoking.

At this moment, on the other side of the English Channel, in London and Bristol and Liverpool, in Manchester and Leeds and Newcastle, in Glasgow and Edinburgh and Aberdeen, in Belfast and Dublin and Limerick, cars are going up in flames, but in slow motion.

IF I COULD

I would
see
want
do
drink a lot more
tick a lot more off
it's dark here
in the middle of my room
the only faint light on the leftmost side
is cast by the empty beer bottle by the window
guitar music starts up

THAT WAS THE FAN BELT

The next morning.

Amazing that it exists. That it keeps coming back, every day it all starts again from the beginning, and then it ends somehow, and then it starts up again. Sometimes I wonder who actually arranged it all like this, and who's paying for it.

We're on the way back to Bremen, Stepanovic, Rocktäschel, Lindner and me. No trace of the woman with the red hair in Hamburg. Stepanovic says we'd better start looking for her in Bremen, in Nouri Saroukhan's past, he thinks that's the only way it'll work, so we do it. The brown Mercedes squeaks and wobbles, and is turning with a groan into the Steintor district, when the fan belt snaps.

'Damn it, Riley,' says Stepanovic, 'if you were wearing tights for once in your life, I could fix this in nothing flat.'

'No tights,' I say, getting out and lighting a cigarette. 'Garage.'

'OK, I'll call the breakdown service,' says Stepanovic as he gets out and lights up too, and pulls out his telephone.

Rocktäschel and Lindner come crawling out of the back seat. And, of course, they also want to smoke. Like teenagers.

The sun is shining, the sky is decorated with little white clouds, as if it were a festival tent.

It's nearly summer.

'So,' says Rocktäschel, 'what now?'

'Two of us take Nouri's primary school on Schmidtstrasse,' I say, 'and two take the Alte Gymnasium.'

'Schmidtstrasse's just round the corner,' says Rocktäschel. 'You and Stepanovic could walk there once the breakdown truck's come. Lindner and I will take a stroll to the Alte Gymnasium, it's not that far to anywhere in Bremen.'

'Good plan,' I say. 'Is that your old school too?'

'No.' He shakes his head. 'I was at the Kippenberg.'

Fag-End Mountain. I choke on my cigarette smoke.

'No laughing.'

'Never, Rocktäschel.'

Stepanovic has finished his telephoning. He throws his cigarette away and lays a hand on the Mercedes' roof.

'Ten minutes and the nice doctor'll be here.'

He gives his car an encouraging kick on the front tyre.

'Have you divvied up the jobs?'

I nod.

'Us two are taking the primary school.'

'Thank God,' he says, 'I always was too stupid for the grammar.'

'When shall we meet up?' asks Lindner; today, he looks more done in than dressed up to any number, and not even vaguely awake; he looks more like someone ran over his face yesterday. A stroll will do him good.

Stepanovic looks at his watch. 'In the afternoon some time,' he says. 'I'll call you when I know when the car will be back on the road.'

'We could take the train back to Hamburg,' says Lindner.

Stepanovic plucks a cloud from the sky, stuffs Lindner into it, lobs him into the nearest corner and shakes his head.

'Take the train. Some people.'

A FACE TO MATCH THE TASTE IN MY MOUTH

And so, the four of us set off in search of a girl who is now a young woman with hair as red as fire. The primary school is at the end of Schmidtstrasse, a dark brick building with white freckles of windows. It looks like a school in a children's book; in fact, the whole road looks like it's fallen out of a book for small people. People who are convinced that everything will always turn out well, or better still, won't even get bad in the first place. There are delicate birch trees outside the school, their soft, pale leaves moving in the wind, just like the wild flowers and rose bushes in the front gardens of the colourfully painted, two-storey houses on either side of the cobblestones.

The headteacher is a friendly woman of about my age, but in a political debate, where I'd put my X in the box marked 'Soviet republic', she'd plump for 'bees and butterflies'.

'I always thought Nouri Saroukhan was a very interesting pupil,' she says, pouring tea for us.

I think: tea, yikes.

'He was clever, quiet, yet he had quite a lot of friends. For such an introverted child.' She sits with us at the table in the middle of her office. She smiles. The wind plays with the chequered curtains hanging by the open window.

'Really, everyone liked him.'

She takes a sip of tea. So do I. Yuk. Stepanovic makes a face to match the taste in my mouth.

'Although he didn't have an easy time of it, of course. I was surprised his parents even let him do his exams.'

'How do you mean?' asks Stepanovic, who's always so good at acting like he hasn't the least idea.

Mrs Headmistress isn't falling for that. She looks sternly at him.

'Oh, come on. You must know perfectly well what kind of household Nouri grew up in.'

Got it. Don't take Bremen for a fool and certainly not the people in this neck of the woods.

She drinks another sip of the tea. 'Would you tell me how he died?'

We tell her.

She looks out of the window, a shadow settles over her face.

'He could really have amounted to something.'

'Could we speak to one of his teachers?' I ask.

'I was his teacher,' she says.

She folds her hands in her lap, the light's gone out in her eyes.

'What exactly do you want to know?'

'Who his friends were,' says Stepanovic. 'Including girls. We are specifically looking for a girl with red hair. Although it's probably dyed, she isn't necessarily a natural redhead. So, a girl he was close friends with, that's who we're looking for.'

She shakes her head.

'I can only think of boys. Wait a moment.'

She stands up and walks to her filing cabinet.

'I'll dig out a few names for you. As far as I know they all still live around here, or else they've moved back. Maybe one of them can help you.'

SOMETHING WENT WRONG

Julius Branding's skateboard shop is where Steintorviertel meets Ostertorviertel, not far from the Saroukhans' house.

Among the colourful boards, trainers and baseball caps, we find a girl. Or rather: a name.

'Aliza Anteli,' says Branding, stroking back his chin-length hair. 'She lived across the Weser, by the Buntentor. Nouri always met up with her on the Stadtwerder.'

He adjusts a couple of boards that are hanging on the wall.

'Back then, we found it funny that he was suddenly such close friends with a girl – that's pretty unusual at that age, isn't it? But there just seemed to be some really strong bond between the two of them. Even idiots like us noticed that. Aliza seemed to be really important to him, somehow.'

'Are you still in touch with her?' asks Stepanovic.

Branding shakes his head. 'I never really was. She and Nouri preferred it just to be the two of them, there was no room for us, which sometimes caused arguments. And then, all of a sudden, she disappeared off the scene. We were at the grammar school by then, we were about fifteen, maybe…? I couldn't say for certain. But it must have been just after the millennium.'

'How do you mean, disappeared off the scene?' I ask.

Branding shrugs. 'Well, yeah, one day she was just gone. Nouri said something about a guy beating her up, he was always talking about it at first, saying she might have ended up in hospital and he had to find her, but then that stopped and he never mentioned her again. She was just gone.'

'What do you think happened?'

'Pff, no idea, I don't know much about those families, I just know it's not much fun for the girls.'

He fiddles with a couple of boards again.

'She probably ran away. Well, if she had any sense, she ran away.'

'How do you mean?' asks Stepanovic, 'those families?'

'Oh, the Lebanese clans,' says Branding, 'or wherever it is they come from. Nouri's family was like that too. What's he doing these days, anyway? I haven't heard from him in ages. Haven't heard from him since he went to Hamburg. Why are you so interested in him and Aliza?'

'Nouri Saroukhan is dead,' says Stepanovic. 'And he was probably killed. We're trying to find out who did it, and why.'

Branding makes a face as though all his boards have dropped off the walls.

'Shit. Shit, whoa, oh man, Nouri. Something in his life went wrong the moment Aliza went away.'

NOURI AND ALIZA, SOMEWHERE IN BETWEEN, MAYBE NIGHT, MAYBE MORNING

At night, he lay awake and missed her. But he also missed her while he slept. He missed her with his eyes open and with them closed, although it was worse when they were closed, because then he saw her everywhere, in every face, at every second.

He had to look for her, he was looking for her all the time anyway. Sometimes, in the early hours of the morning, when he was asleep, he spoke to her in his dreams.

He asked her what she was doing.

She said that she was hiding.

Where? he asked.

Then she just looked at him.

Hang on, he said, I'll hang on though you're gone, and I'll hang in there till you're back.

I'm not coming back, she said, and then her face grew see-through.

He reached for her in his dream, he tried to hold her tight, he tried to explain everything that was, he threw himself into his pillow, and then the pillow started battering him, and then Ali was there, battering everything that moved, and then he saw Melika lying on the road and Aliza running over to Melika and looking at him and saying: you can't do that, not you, you can't do that too.

When he woke up in the mornings, he pulled his diary – in

which he was counting off the days until his exams – out from under his bed. Still eighty-seven days. He crossed off the day ahead. He knew that he wouldn't be able to sleep again until he'd found her.

Then he stood up, got dressed, ate his breakfast in silence, went to school, and hung on.

He wasn't the planning type, but the plan made itself, bit by bit.

HAVE WE GOT A SCREW LOOSE?

'I don't give a crap, we're going in,' says Stepanovic.

He's standing outside the building where Aliza Anteli's family lives. A block of flats on the bustling Buntensteintorweg, its façade is painted dusky pink, the brown window frames look as though it'd be better not to handle them too roughly.

Our colleague Bargfrede gave us the address, and he said it would be better if we didn't go in alone. If he came with us. It would be better not to just confront the Antelis with this Aliza business. There's too much pressure in the cooker there.

It really would be better not to go without him.

In so many words.

But he didn't have time today, he'd come to see the Antelis with us tomorrow.

We all know that we ought to have abided by that, should have, whatever. You just don't mess about in your colleagues' patch. So we're standing suitably diffidently outside the family's door, Rocktäschel, Lindner and me.

Stepanovic buggers that and rings.

No answer.

He rings again.

Nothing.

He rings the neighbours' bell.

'Yes?'

'Open up. Police.'

It buzzes, it clicks, Stepanovic pushes open the front door and we walk up to the fourth floor.

Two doors. One says *Markovic/Schöller*, Stepanovic says 'aha', there's no name by the other door. Outdoor shoes in various sizes are piled on several doormats.

Stepanovic rings.

Still no answer.

'Perhaps there's nobody there,' says Lindner: perhaps he just isn't in the mood for trouble.

Stepanovic taps his forehead. 'Nobody there? 'Sake, Lindner, there are a million shoes outside this door. Bullshit. They're just not answering. I wouldn't either, if I were them and I was at the door.'

He knocks. Loud and clear. A knock that sounds urgent. Along with another: 'Open up. Police.'

Something happens behind the door. Someone's shuffling along, but making it snappy.

Then the door opens.

Then everything happens pretty fast.

The guy is tall, almost as tall as Stepanovic, who easily measures in at six foot three, but, on the other hand, the guy at the door is twice as broad and twice as hard in the face. His head is shaved, his beard is deep black, he's wearing a vest and trackie bottoms, and flip-flops on his feet.

And he yells at us.

Have we got a screw loose?

What's the meaning of all this ringing and knocking?

That his father's sick.

That we should kindly piss off.

Rocktäschel and Lindner have immediately whipped out

their guns and taken a step back. Stepanovic has reached out and put his right hand on the holster.

The gorilla isn't fussed. He carries on yelling and, at some point, I switch off; at some point, Stepanovic shoves his hands in his pockets, turns away and says to the other two: 'Let it go, we're not putting up with this. This place is nuts.'

The gorilla yells at us all the way down the stairs that we're pissing fuckwits.

Once we're outside the front door again, we shake ourselves and light cigarettes for each other. OK, here you go, one for you, one for you, one for you, and now one for me, we're all still here and not in the wrong film.

'Who was that?' I ask, although a better question might be: what was that?

'I reckon,' says Rocktäschel, 'that that was one of Aliza Anteli's brothers. Pleasant fellow. And I'd bet my arse that on the night Saroukhan died, that guy was banged up. That guy wouldn't miss a punch up. There's no talking to him, at any rate.'

He looks at his watch.

'It's just after one. The nearest primary school is just down the road. Aliza must have gone there. If we're lucky, we'll catch someone in the staff room. Maybe we can get something from them.'

Stepanovic nods and looks pleased with Rocktäschel.

That's exactly why he brought him aboard. For this kind of rapid switchover, with local knowledge, when needed.

We throw our cigarettes away and sprint down to the school, and I think: we'd really better listen to Bargfrede next time.

NOURI AND ALIZA: FOUND

He went to the harbour every night.

Every bloody night.

Bridges one to ten, and beyond, he walked from 'Return Again Point' in the middle of the harbour to the Fish Auction Hall, sometimes, when it was raining, he even walked to the beach.

He'd been in Hamburg a year now. No trace of Aliza. Until that night. He was just about to go, bridge seven swayed beneath his feet, but he was used to the swaying, it suited him. Then she came towards him on a black bicycle. He recognised her the moment he saw her, his heart briefly stopped beating, and then it beat all the harder, it caught up on all the beats he'd dropped into the water over the last year.

She got off and walked towards him.

Her face was unchanged, even if it was a little pale. The sun that they'd filled up on together on the island in the Weser had vanished. And her hair was no longer long and black, it was dyed red and rather straw-like from being dyed so often. It looked as though the colour had been stirred up over a fire in a cellar somewhere. But anyone who knew Aliza would recognise her straight away. By her wild eyes, by the rage that burnt within them, by her muscular legs.

She stopped beside him.

He didn't know what he should say.

'So now you're here,' she said.

'Yes,' he said after a while in which he could do nothing but look at her, 'now I'm here.'

She laid her hand on his face, in the middle of his face, and started to cry.

He took her in his arms, he took the bike in his arms too, along with everything else, he took everything there was in his arms, his arms were made of rubber, he wrapped them around her as often as he could.

She spoke into his neck.

Had he got cigarettes.

'Yep,' he said.

Did he have a flat.

'Yep,' he said.

Did he have curtains.

'I've got blinds.'

And she said: 'OK, let's go.'

MIGHT SNAP IN HALF IN THE MIDDLE

Rocktäschel was right. We did indeed find a teacher who taught Aliza Anteli twenty years ago. Now we know: Aliza was born in Bremen on 27th November 1990, the youngest of eight children, a wild girl who came from a heavy-handed home. If she didn't want to come along, her brother just grabbed her by the hair.

She'd never cried.

She'd just always been furious.

She vanished in the summer of 2005, or at least that's what his colleagues at the high school on Leibnizplatz had told him.

Aliza's sister Melika works in a self-service bakery on Buntentorsteinweg, she lives in a bedsit right over the bread shop. Her husband threw her out because she hadn't got pregnant. Her family ignore her and act as if she were dead.

'You should speak to Melika,' the teacher said. 'And please keep me informed about Aliza.' He scribbled his phone number on a piece of paper and slipped it to me. 'I often think about that girl. I'd like to know how she is. And if she's still alive.'

Melika Anteli is sitting with us at a table in the back left-most corner of the bakery. She's brought coffee for us and kind of pastry rings with colourful sprinkles on them. Kiddie food. It took her a long time to arrange everything, one thing at a time, on the table.

She's so thin she might snap in half in the middle if anyone talks too loudly. She's wearing a dark-blue head scarf and a brown, ankle-length dress that's more a kind of coat. No jewellery. She's only just thirty, but her stance is that of a very old woman. She kneads her delicate fingers and doesn't look any of us in the eye.

Stepanovic takes one of the pastries.

'May I?'

'Yes, yes. Of course.'

She raises her head and immediately clings to his gaze.

So, it's between the two of them now. OK.

'Does the name Nouri Saroukhan mean anything to you?'

A smile in a cotton-wool face. One more emotion and it'll shatter.

'Nouri,' she says, and then she seems to be listening to someone talking to her from the far distance. As if she'd suddenly gone on a journey. Then she says: 'How is he?'

Stepanovic won't have the heart to tell her about Nouri's death. I'm curious to know what he'll do.

He just smiles and says nothing.

'Nouri's in Hamburg, isn't he?'

Stepanovic keeps smiling, keeps saying nothing, hints at something that you could interpret as agreement or, then again, not.

'We're looking for your sister Aliza, Ms Anteli,' I say.

She gives me a very fleeting glance, then she's back with Stepanovic.

There's someone in dire need of a protector.

She fishes her purse out of a knackered handbag. She pulls a yellowed photo from the purse and pushes it across the table to Stepanovic.

Her eyes fill with tears at such a rate that I'd like to yell 'stop!'

but the tears get caught behind her eyelids and don't flow. They seem to be stuck to Melika Anteli's soul. As if she'd just vanish into thin air were even her tears to leave her now.

Stepanovic picks up the photo but doesn't pocket it. That kind of thing can go wrong. Pocket it too fast and she'll want it back at once.

'Take a snap of it,' I say quietly and I sound like a machine. 'We can't take it away from her.'

Stepanovic's index finger rests on the photo.

'This is your sister Aliza?'

She nods.

The picture shows a girl with black curls, the curls look un-combed and scraped back into a rudimentary plait. The girl isn't smiling, but there's an exciting twist playing around her mouth, and her dark eyes glow. She looks like someone on fire from the inside. She looks as though she's always thirsty.

'Can I take a photograph of it?' Stepanovic lays his hand on Melika Anteli's constantly kneading fingers. 'Then you can keep the picture.'

She nods, reaches for his hand and pulls on him with her eyes.

I can understand everything she does so well. Just reach very directly for someone for once and pull on him. Either the other person will pull you out or you'll at least no longer be alone in hell.

I wish I could take her with us.

I wish I could run away.

Stepanovic withdraws his hand from hers and takes a photo of the photo.

Then he looks at Melika. 'Why did your sister vanish when she did?'

She starts trembling.

'Could she have disappeared to Hamburg?'

Her tear ducts top up the fluid levels, or maybe it's her heart, she's got a bloody aquarium for eyes now.

'OK,' says Stepanovic.

He puts his phone away, stands up, pulls his chair beside her chair, sits down, and takes her in his arms.

'It's all right.'

He lays his hand on her head.

'Everything's all right.'

I hate it when anyone says everything's all right because everything's never all right, especially for someone like Melika Anteli, when probably nothing in her life has ever come even close to being all right, but I also know that at this particular moment Stepanovic is doing everything right, because perhaps this is the one time in Melika's life in which something really is kind of OK.

Rocktäschel sits beside me and fights with something in his eyes, Lindner shovels down one pastry after another and washes that dry shit down with more and more coffee, as if he had to get something out of his throat.

Later, much, much later, when Stepanovic has let go of Melika Anteli and we're leaving, she stands behind the shop window and waves, and I feel like throwing myself into the Weser at the first opportunity.

Or at least plunging Stepanovic in there.

'I don't know,' I say.

We've marched to the bridge at a stiff pace and now we're standing there and taking a breath. Below us, a pleasure boat chugs over the water.

'I don't know either,' says Stepanovic, 'but I don't know what else I should have done.'

'I'd have done just what you did,' said Lindner, and then I can't help putting my arm around his shoulders.

He beams at me.

'Are we friends now?'

'No.'

NOURI AND ALIZA
BEHIND BLINDS

The flat was small, and it didn't look all that, and Nouri had been a bit embarrassed by it. He'd wanted to offer Aliza a palace when he found her, she damn well deserved a palace.

'Hey, it's fab,' she'd said and thrown herself onto the bed, and the bed hadn't even been made.

He lay down next to her.

They'd never lain together anywhere but the beach before, but it wasn't at all weird to lie with her in bed and look at her.

She smelled of everything except perfume.

She told him what running away had been like, how she'd got off the train in Hamburg at Altona station, the end of the line. How she hadn't known where to go, and how she'd just sat down outside the station. How the people had thought she was begging, and how she'd thought, fine, I'll do that then.

She'd spent a few days like that until someone had turned up, a thin man with short black hair. The man had been very friendly. He'd said that she mustn't stay on the street, and that he could help her, and since then she'd been where the man was.

'Where's that?' asked Nouri, playing with her hand.

'Doesn't matter,' she said. 'It's safe. I think. They're nice. They help me and I help them. I've got everything I need.'

'I have too now,' he said, and then he told her about her sisters.

About Melika who was having to fend for herself lately because his brother was such an arsehole. About the other sisters that you sometimes saw in the supermarket, they walked with a stoop, and they only spoke when they were starting an argument with someone.

Something glittered in Aliza's eyes.

He briefly considered telling her about his legal studies, but then he didn't bother and stroked her shaggy hair.

She didn't like it.

'Can I have a shower here?'

'Sure,' he said, and she stood up and undressed, that was just how she was, she didn't give a damn what other people thought, and when she dropped her clothes on the floor, the reinforced concrete across the whole city trembled.

She looked like a warrior.

IMMIGRANT KIDS

Rocktäschel and Lindner have taken the train back to Hamburg. Rocktäschel had had enough of Bremen for today, and in the end, Lindner always wants what Rocktäschel wants.

Stepanovic and I wait by the river for the Mercedes to be back on the road. Seven p.m., the mechanic said.

The Weser's not the Elbe, but it's OK.

A river that you can look at.

When it comes down to it, the Weser is perfectly adequate.

Water that flows.

Ships that travel from A to B on the water, sometimes with a bit of industry thrown in.

Quay walls that you can sit on.

Gulls, even the big ones.

This works, I think, and I say: 'This works.'

'What does?'

Stepanovic lets his legs dangle and smokes.

'Us sitting here now like this.'

'Yes,' he says. 'This works pretty well.'

I light a cigarette too.

'I tried to call Calabretta just now. He didn't answer.'

'They're still busy interviewing people at AKTO,' says Stepanovic. 'But he told me yesterday that they'd probably be finished with them all this evening.'

'What do you reckon he'll concentrate on?'

'We ought to finally get the forensics report tomorrow morning,' he says. 'The guys didn't have an easy job because the car was so carbonised. But they might have found some indication of who set the thing on fire.'

'And what do you think?'

He drags on his cigarette. Looks at the water. Ponders.

'I don't think this murder is a classic case of clan criminality or an outbreak of gang warfare or whatever,' he says. 'The guys from organised crime say there's absolutely no sign that the Mhallami families, or the Saroukhans in particular, want to check in to Hamburg. Round our way, the Hells Angels are so firmly in the red-light driving seat, and they're so strong, that it would cost much too much energy to get involved there.'

'There'd be deaths,' I say.

'Evidently, the gentlemen here are relatively unfazed by deaths. But they're not dumb. They've got everything they need in Bremen, Lower Saxony and North-Rhine Westphalia. Why should they suddenly try to plough loads of effort and money into being players in Hamburg's underworld, which has always been fiercely competitive anyway? And when you can already predict that it probably wouldn't work out? They'd rather take the nice, comfortable route and expand into Holland or Belgium or somewhere.'

He stubs his cigarette out on the cobbles and lights another.

I watch a gull that seems to be chasing something.

'If this isn't inter-clan stuff, what is it then?'

'I have the feeling that it still could be someone from Nouri's family,' he says. 'Seeing what they're like, I wouldn't put much past them. Or it was one of the Antelis. OK, so Bargfrede says that Mohamed and Tarek were in police custody with the others at the time of the incident, and they're Aliza's only two brothers, but there are heaps of cousins too. I asked him to have another look at anyone who wasn't actually banged up that night, and if any of them are possibilities. Something happened between Nouri and Aliza that got them both into difficulties.'

There's another gull at our feet, fighting a swan over a piece of stale bread.

Stepanovic chucks his cigarette in the river.

'You're so anti-social, Ivo.'

'And you're an immigrant kid, Riley.'

'So are you.'

The gull flies off with the bread in its beak.

NOURI AND ALIZA AT THE HARBOUR

The end of bridge ten was where they always sat. On a bench with a view of the water to the west. On the summer solstice, the light only vanished just before midnight, and around half past two it crawled up again in the east, at their backs.

They sat there as often as they could, but never before twilight. They mostly met on Mondays, Tuesdays and Wednesdays; from Thursday onwards there were too many tourists at the harbour. Too many people. You just never knew who might see you.

Outside, they just met to talk.

For touching they went to Nouri's.

'My brother's dead,' he said.

'Which one? Ali?'

A cloud scudded over her brow.

'Younes,' he said.

'Younes? The little one?'

'He was sixteen.'

An illegal car race at the Weserhafen, just two hours earlier. Sharif's son had forced Younes off, he'd crashed into a container, Nouri had kind of thought the two of them had been friends, but they can't have been. Younes was forced off deliberately.

Said Nouri's father.

'He wants me to come back to Bremen,' said Nouri. 'Because there's going to be war between us and Sharif's family. My dad says Sharif won't accept the arbitrator he picks, on principle.'

'And?' Aliza stared at the water. 'Are you going back to Bremen?'

'I'm going early tomorrow. I want to see Younes again before they bury him.'

Aliza pulled out a packet of tobacco, rolled herself a cigarette, lit it, stared at the water.

'Your brother won't be buried that soon; he'll wind up in the morgue until they work out exactly what happened. But nobody will talk. So he'll stay in the morgue.'

'They'll want him to be buried within forty-eight hours.'

'Exactly,' she said, drew the smoke deep into her lungs, blew it out again, wrapped herself in it. 'There'll be massive trouble.'

She looked at him.

'Don't go, Nouri.'

He took a drag on her cigarette.

'I'm going. But I'll come back.'

'Maybe I won't still be here by then.'

PULL OVER AND GET IT ON

The Mercedes has a new fan belt now, but that doesn't mean that it's stopped squealing. We saunter down the autobahn towards Hamburg at a leisurely pace. Of course, the repair took longer than expected. We've had the sunset at our backs for ages. And every metre we travel has its background concert of squeaks.

'It's the tyres, isn't it?'

Stepanovic nods, winds down his window and lights cigarettes for us. He hands me my fag, then he turns up the radio. Someone's playing the violin.

'Ah, kitsch,' he says, 'plus evening sun. Plus my favourite colleague at my side.' He glances over at me. 'One for the road?' Fag in the corner of his mouth.

'Hey, you're the police.'

'The prosecution doesn't need to find out about it.'

'OK,' I say, 'the prosecution's too tired to find out about anything. Stop at the next services. I'll buy you one for the road.'

'You're so cool, Riley.'

'Are you sure?'

'You can rely on my feelings!'

I look at him.

He's probably right.

I wish I was like that.

Something with feelings you can rely on.

There are no more violins on the radio. A couple of cars are burning in Tokyo. There's a service station up ahead.

Drive up, walk in, walk out again with two cans of beer.

Click.

Fizz.

'Aahhh.'

Stepanovic is the cold-beer-from-a-can type. You can only drink canned beer with dignity if you know what rain in the gutter tastes like. And Stepanovic knows stuff like that because he grew up behind Frankfurt's South Station.

I open a beer for me too, but the click and fizz aren't half as good as my colleague's, although perhaps that's just my imagination.

'Hey, Riley, that ultra-mysterious friend, the one the guys picked up at the airport the other night, is he the one from Istanbul? The one everyone's always talking about? The cop whose arm was ripped off by an Albanian Molotov cocktail?'

I take a swig of my cold beer and a dry drag on my cigarette.

'Yes,' I say. 'The very same.'

'And?'

'And what?'

'Are you and he...?'

Offended now, slamming doors. That's it.

'We were once. But only kind of halfway.'

'What do you mean, only kind of halfway?'

'I wimped out.'

'How come?'

'He wanted to marry me.'

'Wow, the guy's a thrill-seeker.'

'Bullshit.'

We drive and smoke and drink canned beer.

Then him again. 'And, obviously, you didn't want to. Get married, I mean.'

'Why are you interested in all this?'

'I'm not interested. I just like chatting to you. You know, I'm always a bit bored if I can't chat to you.'

'OK.'

I look out of the window.

He looks over at me.

'So. You didn't want to get married.'

'I'm not really the wedding sort. And there was someone else.'

'No way. Seriously?'

'Yeah, but he left around the time you and I met.'

He takes his hands off the wheel. 'That wouldn't have mattered, I'd have got it on with you anyway!'

'Hands on the wheel, Ivo. And us two didn't get it on.'

'True. Why the hell not?'

'No time.'

'Maybe we should just pull over now and get it on?'

'Ivo.'

'I'm only asking.'

He blows smoke into his own eye.

'I don't want anything to get lost in the ether with us.'

'Nothing will get lost, don't worry.' I take his cigarette butt off him and chuck it out of the window. 'If I want to get it on with you, you'll notice.'

'Promise?'

'Promise.'

We drive.

Then the beer runs out.

'What d'you reckon? Another OK?'

'Another's OK.'

I reach behind me to the back seat and pull another two cans round to the front, open them and give one of them to my driver.

'So, what's the deal with the bloke now?'

Whoa.

Man.

'With what bloke?'

'The guy from Istanbul.'

'No idea. Hurts.'

'Still, or again?'

'Both.'

'Then just go to bed with him; that generally helps with that kind of pain.'

If I'm reading things correctly, Stepanovic sleeps with a different woman every night. If he's not in some pub, whacking himself around the head with time till the early hours.

'You're such a fucking love guru, aren't you?'

He grins at me, but it's not a sleazy grin. It's a grin that's so attractive that now and then I do actually find myself thinking about pulling over with him, while we're on the road like this.

'There's a layby coming up,' he says, 'if you want to work with the professionals for a change.'

'Knock it off, Ivo...'

He's about to start.

'...and no dirty jokes now, please.'

He looks at the road and muses a bit to himself, nodding now and again, and then he has an idea: 'Listen up. I'll drive you to that sexy cripple. You two get drunk. And then wait and see what happens.'

'We've been doing that all the time since he got back,' I say. 'Nothing happens to make it better. Except that we can bear it better together than alone.'

'Hang on, sweetheart, I'm not finished.'

Oh right, he's not finished.

'Just take a very precise look at whether or not you want to nail him to the wall...'

'Ivo.'

'...and if nothing comes of it...'

'Ivo...'

'...you can call me, and the two of us can finally do it.'

'Ivo!'

'Chastity!'

LAY YOUR HEAD IN MY SAND

No, Ivo. Just because you offer me sex doesn't mean I'll go along with any old shit deal.

OK.

I wouldn't swear to it now.

Let a few more years go by.

But until then, let's sit on this beach that wasn't dragged here by the river but by human hands, lay your head in my sand, I'll smoke marijuana with you till the sun comes up, 'cos that works too.

IT'S STRANGE BUT THIS ISN'T THE FIRST TIME THIS HAS HAPPENED TO ME

Forensics have found a few interesting things in the charred Fiat. Including DNA.

One female and two males, one of them being Nouri Saroukhan.

'The woman was Aliza Anteli,' says Stepanovic, who seems pretty fixated on this girl now.

'If that's true,' says Calabretta, 'couldn't she be not just a witness but also a suspect?'

'First, we've got to find her,' says Stepanovic, 'and then we'll see what she qualifies as.'

'And who was the guy sitting in the car with Nouri?' I ask, realising that I'm talking about a murder victim as if he were an old friend. That's strange but this isn't the first time this has happened to me.

Calabretta looks at me. 'Finding that out is our task for today.'

'As for us,' says Stepanovic, looking at Rocktäschel and Lindner, 'we'll have a nice time running around the city with the photo of Aliza Anteli. Where shall we start?'

He looks over to me.

'I've got something to check on, so I'm out. But didn't that colleague of Nouri's say the two of them always met down at the harbour?'

NOURI AND ALIZA ON A SHIP, PORTSIDE, ASTERN

On the few occasions when they did meet in the daytime, it was only ever aboard a ship. They mostly sat on the left at the back, on the steps leading up to the deck. If anyone came along and wanted to use the steps, they stopped talking and stood up, and Aliza vanished to the loo.

Sometimes the wind was strong, and then the waves in the port were high: so high that the spray caught them on the steps. Then they had brackish water in their faces. Nouri always wiped it away at once, Aliza never did. When the water caught him that day, he left it where it was. He'd had a visit the evening before. From his brother Ali.

It had been late when Ali had knocked on his door, almost night-time, Nouri had been about to go to bed. He'd known from the knock that it had to be Ali, his brother was the only person who knocked like that, as if only he had the right to knock on doors at all. His brother never rang the bell. His brother always knocked.

Nouri had opened up and asked what was the matter.

Ali had been sent by their father to fetch Nouri home. Nouri's place was now with his family, Ali had said, sitting down at Nouri's table. Nouri had asked what exactly was about to kick off, and Ali had said that the war against Sharif and his family was about to kick off, that the blood had to flow, that it was a matter of family honour, his little brother's honour. When he'd said that, he'd put his feet up on Nouri's table.

'And what did you say?' asked Aliza, wiping a little of the spray off Nouri's forehead.

The ferry jolted against the waves.

'I said that he could sod off with his war.'

Ali had then taken his feet off the table and stood up and then asked if Nouri would say that again.

Nouri had indeed said it again, and followed up by adding that they could all sod off with their war. That he considered the war idiotic. That Younes had died because they always had these fucking wars in their heads, and that another war wouldn't bring him back to life.

Nouri had expected Ali to flip.

But Ali hadn't flipped.

Ali had just looked at him for a long time.

Then he had asked if he should tell their father that.

Nouri had said that Ali could tell their father whatever he liked.

'And then?' asked Aliza, and the spray hit their faces again.

Then Ali had kicked over Nouri's table and left, slamming the door violently behind him, and shouted from the stairwell that he'd be back.

'They'll cast you out,' said Aliza.

'So what if they do?' said Nouri.

'You need money for your degree,' said Aliza.

Nouri wiped the spray off his face and then took Aliza's hands.

'I don't need a degree. I only need you. I can earn money. And then we'll go away.'

'Where will we go?'

'To Mexico,' he said, and she said: 'It's called Mehico.'
It was a bit like that time back in the Kids' Wilderness.

PERSONAL INJURY

The Police Museum is right behind the HQ, in an old building, surrounded by the police academy barracks, and then there
are those flats with the numbers. Faller's waiting for me at the
door, and smoking.

'There you are, my girl.'

'You said I should come.'

'If you're here, it'll help him get started.'

'He doesn't need me.'

'You've got no idea what kind of crazy things an injured man
needs, Chas.'

I light myself a cigarette too.

Faller says: 'You shouldn't smoke so much.'

'For my nerves.'

'And there was me thinking you didn't have any.' He stubs
out his cigarette in the big ashtray installed by the door. 'I'll go
on ahead, then, so it doesn't look as though we've arranged to
meet.'

'We did arrange to meet, Faller.'

He pushes back his hat. 'You'll find us upstairs, OK?'

'OK.'

I take a few steps up and down outside the building with its
old-fashioned plaster. Everywhere round here smells like police
in the old days. Of Black Marias. It's probably the walls.

When I've finished my smoke, I walk up, the stairs creak under my boots.

Bülent Inceman is standing with his back to me in a dark room between Fritz Honka's saws and the Hitler diaries. There are dark-blue walls, thick velvet curtains and glowing orange lights.

His black hair is no longer glossy. He's had it shaved off.

'Ah,' I say, 'change of style.'

He turns around. His face is clear and hard, his crystalline gaze penetrates into every corner of me.

'I represent the force now.'

'You're actually doing the PR?'

'I'm sure he's already told you that,' he says, looking at Faller, who is standing at the other end of the room and having a conversation with a man in a perfectly fitting, cornflower-blue suit. Or rather: Faller's talking, the man is listening politely. He's wearing his hair as short as Inceman does lately, along with a neatly clipped red-blond beard and cognac-coloured stitched ankle boots.

'My new boss,' says Inceman.

'My new style icon,' I say.

'Yeah, the guy looks pretty good.'

You look good, I think.

And those damn lashes.

Fuck.

'So,' I say. 'What kind of a great place have you got here then? Show me your stuff, Mr Press Spokesman.'

'I like the Steindamm hostage situation best,' he says, 'tall gangster tales from the seventies. Over there, come on.'

I feel eyes on the back of my neck – Faller and the museum boss, they're watching us secretly the whole time, while pretending to have something important to discuss – but because they're friendly eyes, it's OK.

Inceman and I watch a film that's running in a constant loop on a small screen. There are policemen in green uniforms; the uniforms look like casual clothes. Short shirts, little badge on the chest, cap on, flares. But soon they'll have to shoot a hostage-taker in the head, and you can see in their faces that, after that, nothing will ever be the same as before. We watch for a long time as the people in the film fight for their composure and a lot more besides.

'All of us here are a bit like them,' says Inceman. 'Something's happened to all of us that's taken a notch out of us. That can't be repaired. Faller's idea of parking me in the museum was spot on.'

'Nobody has the intention of parking you,' I say, and of course I know how that sounds.

'Stop it,' he says, 'it's OK. It really is OK here. We're salvaged, there's something to do, it helps. The guy on the first floor who puts the kids in the helicopter simulator was in Kosovo for too long. Now he's here and it works.'

'And your boss?'

'Former art-theft expert. Interesting guy.'

'Injury?'

'I haven't found out yet,' he says. 'But there's always something. I'll tell you as soon as I know.'

'Will you show me the rest?'

'Sure. What would you like to do first?'

'Fly the helicopter.'

NOURI AND ALIZA IN THE CARETAKER'S FLAT IN THE UNIVERSITY CELLAR

For Nouri, there was something almost ritual about bidding farewell to the uni, it was another step away from everything they wanted from him, and he wanted to celebrate that step with Aliza.

They celebrated in the caretaker's flat.

The caretaker was a friend of Nouri's, an old man who'd once been a professional footballer, till the thing with his knee happened, and then at some point he'd simply become the uni caretaker. When Nouri was new at the uni, the caretaker had seen that he was alone, and he'd taken him under his wing. Sometimes he did that with freshers.

The flat was for emergencies, for caretaking emergencies obviously, but because they'd already broken all the rules they'd grown up with anyway, they didn't care, and Nouri knew where the key was kept.

They stayed for exactly two hours.

They unrolled the large, old map of the world that the caretaker had rescued from a bin after the geography materials were digitised.

They lay on the map and had sex with each other, once on Asia and once on South America, they were just trying it out to see what felt better, and once again they realised that it would be South America where they wanted to live one day.

Aliza briefly spoilt the game by remarking that, unfortunately, she wouldn't be able to go anywhere because she didn't have a passport. The passport had stayed back in Bremen, she'd had no idea of where to look for her papers, she hadn't known if she even had a passport, if she officially existed.

Nouri wasn't going to let her spoil the game.

'My brothers'll get a passport for you, no problem,' he said, and then Aliza started laughing, but the laughter tasted of dust.

When they left the caretaker's flat again, when Nouri turned the key and pulled it out, he told Aliza that he was starting work in an insurance company the next day.

'I'll earn money for us now,' he said, 'and believe me, we'll deal with the passport business somehow.'

He looked at her for a long time.

'I mean that seriously.'

Aliza said: 'I'll walk you there.'

LONELINESS IS LIKE A JACKET THAT'S TOO TIGHT, BUT WITHOUT THE JACKET YOU FREEZE

In any kind of official environment, the common room is fundamentally the roughest space you can enter. A table that's much too large, around it some discarded chairs with challenging cushion covers. An old, roll-fronted cabinet with uncooled drinks.

It's best just to drink red wine.

We're sitting on the floor below one of the old lattice windows, the bottle moving back and forth between us. We're already on to the second, my head is slowly growing heavy.

Inceman puts his left arm around me.

'I've still got *one*,' he says.

Well then, I think, and I scoot closer to him.

He swigs the wine.

'You're lonely, huh?'

'It doesn't necessarily get better with time,' I say. 'But maybe that's how I want it anyway.'

'It's like a jacket that's too tight,' he says. 'But you know that if you take the jacket off, you'll freeze.'

'You always were the pragmatic type.'

'That's changed too,' he says. 'Probably down to the morphine. If you take that stuff, there's somehow no point to anything anymore, you don't care, it's just about the pain. If that's gone, the rest is OK too.'

'Does that mean that if we got to know each other now, you wouldn't try to marry me anymore?'

'What's the point of marrying?'

'Then let's get to know each other,' I say.

He looks at me. 'Is there a problem if you stay here tonight?'

'Here? In the common room? No.'

'There's no one who'd want to smash my face in?'

'No.'

'How about you?'

'I'm not intending to smash your face in.'

He takes another swig from the bottle.

'The wine's nearly finished.'

I take the bottle from him, drain it and say: 'Then we'd better do something else now.'

He looks at me and I can see in his eyes that he's got nothing against a change to the schedule.

It's years since I went to bed with him, and even if there's no bed here, just shabby common room carpeting, the very same thing happens that always used to happen between us when we really pulled out all the stops: as if there were a hurricane inside me that sweeps away anything and everything that isn't nailed down.

So, Stepanovic, you're on, come on, let a dirty joke fly.

STAND BY ME,
BECAUSE OF THE FROGS, AND BECAUSE OF ALL THE
VERY DIFFERENT SHIT TOO

Inceman says that maybe we could both use some therapy.

Not that he's seriously thinking about it. But that, you know, there are people who find that stuff helpful.

I say that the thing I find helpful is if everything just is the way it is. If the world's the case, and if I can at least vaguely rely on it being the case.

He says that he just wanted to have said it. Because of his morphine and all my very different shit.

I say: Well then.

He says: Stay with me.

I light a cigarette and then it starts raining, all kinds of things fall out of the sky, cats, dogs, dragons, knives, even a couple of frogs, and I say: 'Where else would I go?'

KNICKER-RIPPING STORIES

'Could you just pack your silly grin away?'

'My grin isn't silly.'

'OK. Could you pack your normal grin away?'

'What is it about my grin that bothers you?'

'The subtext.'

'I'm not saying anything.'

'Exactly, Ivo. You're not saying anything. But you want to say something. So just spit it out and have done.'

Stepanovic and I are standing outside the police head-quarters, smoking. It's raining sideways.

He glances at me briefly then watches the rain again. Very interesting. Drops. Lots of drops.

'How was sex with your Turkish Travolta?'

'He's not a Turkish Travolta.'

Dripping, raining, *bam, bam, bada-bada boom*.

'He used to be though, didn't he? At least that's what the murder squad guys say. They say he was the sharpest suit of the lot of them.'

Stepanovic drags on his cigarette and tries a whole new facial expression, something between indifferent and serious, with results that could pass for Winston Churchill's grandmother.

'You're a bunch of old women, Ivo. Haven't you got anything better to do than gossiping?'

He shrugs his shoulders and sticks his hands in his trouser pockets. Fag in the corner of his mouth.

'It's only because we all secretly fancy you.'

I pull a face.

There's a blast from the past.

'Come on, Riley. How was it?'

'Paralympic love, classification: broken hearts,' I say and stub my cigarette out in the large, grey, floor-standing ashtray, which could hardly be uglier. It goes perfectly with the weather, which is getting more abusive by the second. The wind whips the water down the steps to the car park, a succession of kicks up the arse.

'And how does he manage it, with only one arm? I mean, really, you can only be on top and he—'

'Hell, Ivo!'

It takes me every trick in the north-German wind-defence book to light a new cigarette.

'I mean, is the guy some kind of superhero? Does he have superhuman powers, or what? Can he fly? Anything like that?'

'He used to be a superhero,' I say. 'Now he's half a superhero. But that's more than enough for me. After all, he's still got a whole shoulder.'

I smoke.

'Over and out.'

Stepanovic nods, he seems to be thinking. Imagining something.

'Why don't you just pop back upstairs?' I say. 'Maybe you and Calabretta could read a few knicker-ripping novels together, if the subject interests you that much.'

'That would suit you,' he says, and lights yet another cigarette, the wind drops for two seconds, the flame of his lighter stands enviably still in the air.

'I'll stay right here.'

Five minutes later, we get into the lift. My body is still remembering how things were last night, but we're both actually in the process of forgetting it again.

Stepanovic briefly touches my hand.

'Don't worry, Riley, you're safe with me.'

Then the lift spits us out.

LOST THE TELEPHONE NUMBER

Anne Stanislawski stands with pen at the ready by the white board, which is by now completely covered in writing. Everything that we know about Nouri Saroukhan and his life in Bremen and Hamburg. The one picture we have of Aliza Anteli stuck next to the various photos we have of Nouri.

I lob a 'good morning' into the ring and sit down at the large desk. My colleagues mumble something back and their eyes dart around the room. Stepanovic sits down beside me.

'What's the news from AKTO?' he asks.

'We're still talking to Marcel Thomforde,' says Anne Stanislawski, 'the only one of his colleagues that Nouri was sort of friends with. He had no social contact with any of the others. And we're trying to find out what kind of guy Marco Cardoso is – the boss in that place. He comes across as kind of creepy, at least to me.'

She points with her pen at the photos, shot from the hip, of two men who look totally average, yet as though someone had poured varnish over them. Their hair is so unnaturally shiny. The guys look almost a bit like investment bankers – all they're missing is the class. There's something not quite right about their shirt collars. And the smaller of the two looks decidedly nicer than the other.

'At the moment, Thomforde's our best conversationalist,' says

Calabretta. 'He doesn't hold back about the pretty strained atmosphere at AKTO, and he does seem to have known quite a
lot about Nouri's state of mind. Something was bothering him
recently, apparently. Thomforde says he had the feeling that
Nouri was on the point of telling him something important.
But there's no evidence of anything unusual, either on his computer or in his diary.'

'Have you been able to get hold of his mobile phone yet?'

Calabretta shakes his head. 'Gone.'

'And what does the boss, this Cardoso, have to say about
Nouri's death?'

'Nothing in particular,' says Stanislawski, shaking her head.
'In any case, we won't get anything out of him that will make
much sense. He's primarily concerned with himself, and looks
as though he refuels on compressed air every morning.'

'And he's snorting his nose away morning, noon and night,'
says Brückner. 'Glass eyes.'

'Mind you, looking at the other blokes there,' says
Stanislawski, 'he's not the only one. The pressure seems to be
immense. They only talk about figures and bonuses, even with
us, as if this stuff is all they ever talk about to anyone, and
parked outside the door is a fleet of cars that would be right at
home in filthy-rich Innocentia Park, and all the stuff that
happens always happens at an incredible pace: even the women
in the porn they watch in between times get shagged quicker
than anywhere else.'

The men in the room look at her with raised eyebrows.

'What?' she says. 'I stole a glance over their shoulders.'

'I'd like to pop round and see this place,' I say.

'We've got a meeting with Thomforde in his office in two
hours,' says Calabretta. 'And we're asking the gentlemen for a vol-

untary DNA test today. But they think we're so shit that I don't expect to get anyone but Thomforde and maybe Marco Cardoso to spit on a cotton bud.' He puffs out his cheeks. Whew.

'A search warrant for the whole office would be ideal, wouldn't it?' I say.

First Calabretta nods, then he shakes his head, and then he says: 'But we've got nothing to go on. No suspicions. The best we could do would be to fetch the drugs squad and act like they're in charge now. Get in through the back door, so to speak.'

'Just tell me when you guys need what by way of paperwork,' I say. 'And I'll get on to it for you.'

'OK. Thanks.' He smiles. 'What shall we do next about the girl?'

'Rocktäschel and Lindner have been out and about in the city with the photo since yesterday,' says Stepanovic. 'Today they sent it out to all stations, across a wide area; they're at the Davidwache station at the moment, putting a team together focused entirely on finding Aliza Anteli. But for the time being, we're being cautious; we're not launching a massive hunt just yet. Don't want to drive her even further underground when she's already missing.'

'You think Aliza's the key, don't you?' asks Schulle, playing with a strand of blond hair that's fallen from his parting into his face.

'I'd just love to talk to her,' says Stepanovic. 'And I have the feeling that Saroukhan's death has more to do with his family than this insurance company you're so crazy about right now. But either way: if Aliza is the woman I saw on top of the multi-storey on Mexico Street, she might have seen who set fire to Nouri's car. And it was presumably her who called the fire brigade.'

'It was definitely a woman's voice,' says Anne Stanislawski, 'although quite deep. I've listened to the emergency call a few times now. The voice sounded strangely calm and composed. That doesn't really fit with someone who was very close to the victim, does it?'

'If Aliza's gone through what we think she's gone through,' I say, 'there won't be much that'll shock that woman. She can handle a lot.'

'Or she started the fire herself,' says Calabretta quietly, although somehow, I don't like that idea.

Stepanovic stands up and stretches. 'I'd like to bring someone else in on our clan investigation, someone with more direct access to the scene. The organised crime guys say there's no Mhallami activity here yet, but we ought to sound that out on the ground. With someone who knows their way around on the ground better than any kind of police.'

Embarrassed silence.

Even last summer, Klatsche would've been the guy to kind of bring in right now. But Klatsche's not here anymore.

And I've stupidly lost his telephone number.

'Faller?' asks Calabretta.

Stepanovic nods.

'He's still got contacts, hasn't he? And he can bring in whoever he likes. Then it's nothing to do with us.'

'I'll call him right away,' I say.

'Or you could just call in, round at the Police Museum,' says Stepanovic with such a stupid grin that I have a really urgent desire to kick him in the kidneys.

Everyone else has a grin too, Anne Stanislawski blushes a little.

The tosspots really have been talking about me all morning. Unbelievable.

'Bite me,' I say.
Then I go and make a phone call.

ARE YOU STILL EATING THAT?

The rain has transformed into impenetrable, heavy cloud, the wet lies around on the streets and on people's heads, nothing can scare it away; the wind has taken its leave too.

Faller and I are standing under the awning at a Thai snack kiosk, smoking while we wait for the spicy stuff we've ordered to arrive. He pushes back his hat.

'Ask around, uh-huh,' says Faller.

'Ask around,' I say.

'Where exactly?'

'You know that better than me.'

'This isn't to do with Klatsche?'

I drag on my cigarette.

Breathe.

'No,' I say. 'It's nothing to do with Klatsche. Just criminal clans.'

'Thank God for that,' he says. 'Otherwise it would have been way too delicate even for me.'

The snack-bar woman brings two bowls of soup and puts them down on the table in front of us. The soup steams, it's piping hot and red, and there are little green chillies swimming on the surface.

'Does that mean you'll help us?'

Faller has leant over his bowl, he's stirring his soup, blows first here then there.

'Of course I'll help you. I think I know who to talk to.' He looks me in the eye across the table. 'But it's none of your business, OK?'

'That's the deal,' I say and take a spoonful of my soup. Wow, it's hot. 'There's another thing.'

He lowers his spoon and smiles paternally. 'I really don't care at all what you and Mr Inceman get up to, my girl.'

He clearly does care. He seems to be thrilled to bits that we're getting up to something, whatever that may be. He hasn't given up hope of me finding a home again. Or else he's just scared that one day I'll move in with him.

'A business matter,' I say.

'Oh right.'

That's just boring.

He turns his attention back to his soup.

I pull out a print-out of the photo of Aliza Anteli that I swiped from the police HQ and lay it on the table.

'We're looking for this girl. She must be in her late twenties now, and her hair is probably not black anymore but bright red.'

Faller lets his spoon sink back into his soup. 'Who's this wild thing?'

'She comes from a Mhallami family and probably ran away from Bremen in 2005,' I say. 'We think she's in Hamburg. And she might know who killed Nouri Saroukhan, the young man who died in his car.'

'Is she in danger?'

'Could be. But she could also *be* the danger, or at least Calabretta's thinking along those lines. Stepanovic and I see it differently, but hopefully time will tell. If you know anyone who could be shown the picture, just do it, OK?'

He pushes his soup bowl away and nods. He takes the

picture, sticks it in his jacket pocket and his hand rests there beside it for a moment. I can see that Aliza's face has stirred something within him. He's got a soft spot for lost girls.

'Don't you like the soup, Faller?'

'It's too hot for me.'

'I can see that.'

I eat another couple of spoonfuls and then my stomach's had enough of the chillies too.

'Will you come over to the museum again?'

It's too hot for me, I think.

'I can't, I'm busy.'

Faller straightens his hat, pulls it deeper over his face. 'Shall I say hi to him?'

'What for?'

We part. I watch him walk away for a few minutes – I like his walk so much. Broad steps. Like a sailor on shore leave.

On the way back to the station, I pass the newspaper stand at a U-Bahn kiosk. Old cars have been burning in Africa for days.

CUPBOARDS WITH TEETH, AIR MADE OF GRANITE

Car Maintenance, Engine Diagnosis, Accident Repairs.

That's what it says on the door to a concrete skyscraper that seems to be concerned exclusively with cars. Right opposite, outside the door to AKTO Insurance, are the wheels to match.

Calabretta, the murder squad's petrolhead, reels them off: 'Audi A6 Competition, three hundred and twenty-six hp, awesome for someone a bit younger. Five Series BMW M, four hundred hp, pure adrenaline under your arse. Porsche Panamera Turbo S E-Hybrid, oh wow, I'd love that, man. Porsche Cayenne, I'm not really into that SUV shit, they all look the same, jacked-up OAP cars: BMW X-5, pah, Range Rover Evoque, nah, Alfa Romeo Stelvio, oh, Alfa, I dunno. Jaguar F-Pace. Well. OK. Maybe that one's not so bad, especially in blue. Ah, here, Mercedes Benz. S-Class AMG Coupé. Now that's a car, guys.'

I look at the other three. 'Does he do this every time you turn up here?'

'Every pissing time,' says Anne Stanislawski. 'I'll be able to recite the cars off by heart myself soon.'

The gleaming black Mercedes is only very distantly related to Stepanovic's clapped-out brown thing. In point of fact, there isn't the least similarity between the two models.

Team Old Merc.

I always find new cars so brash.

'The S-Class belongs to the chief,' says Schulle, who's gone as misty-eyed as his boss in the face of the large expanse of polished metal.

'Hey, has he put fatter boots on it?' asks Calabretta, crossing his arms over his chest. As if he were insulted at not having been informed.

Schulle shakes his head and says: 'Nah, it just kind of looks like it, maybe because of the rain or something, that can cause sort of optical illusions on the tarmac…'

He worships the Mercedes, he can hardly think.

The motors seem to leave Brückner rather colder.

'Shall we go in, then?'

'Sure, guys, come on,' says Calabretta. 'We're not here for fun, are we?'

Mmm.

Exactly.

AKTA's Hamburg North office is on the ground floor of a business bunker in gilt-mirrored glass and red-painted washed concrete. Calabretta leads the way, the door slides open automatically, we walk behind him.

There are room dividers in the open-plan office to give the staff the feeling that some thinking's been done here. Little groups of men in suit trousers are standing between the plasterboard panels. Their jackets are hanging over swivel chairs, none of which seem to belong to a desk; the few tables standing around in the cubicles are largely empty, now and then there's a telephone or one of those clear plastic storage crates on one. The men have rolled up their shirtsleeves, their ties are a fraction too tight around their throats, their neck muscles ooze out of their collars. They look at us as if they were a warrior horde and we were something else.

They move their lower jaws, some of them stop blinking.

Purple carpet, testosterone up to the ceiling, air made of granite. Corporate identity.

'Our friends and helpers are back again,' says the only one who seems to have a proper workplace; at least, he's sitting at a fully equipped desk with a computer, and filing and telecommunications systems.

Officer on the bridge.

'Mornin',' says Calabretta. Then he walks over to a more delicate-looking man with short dark-blond hair – the only one who isn't standing around like a cupboard with teeth. 'Mr Thomforde. Good of you to make time for us again.'

'Yes, Marcel,' says the guy at the head waiter's desk, 'that strikes me as noteworthy too.' He's snarking at Thomforde. 'Can't have anything else to do, huh?'

Thomforde doesn't react to the pissing from the sidelines and shakes hands with us all.

I introduce myself as briefly as possible.

The boss stands up but makes no effort to leave his position of power to come and greet us.

'Marco Cardoso,' he says, looking at me. 'I'm the responsible adult here.'

And he must indeed be ten years older than the rest. He's got black hair, neatly cut and combed and sprayed back precisely; his angular, clean-shaven chin gleams; and his tie contains at least as much keratin as his grooming products.

All his employees here, that much is clear.

'Chastity Riley,' I say again, straightening up. 'Prosecution service.'

I can do display behaviour too, sweetie-pie.

Let me get a head count.

Eleven men, one whole football team. There are nine cars outside. So I bet two of them have lost their licences. Jumping lights, doing 240 down the motorway, aggressive driving, whatever, doesn't take much to forfeit the things these days. And nobody here would voluntarily get the bus to work.

'So, which of you lot is currently waiting to get his driving licence back?' I ask.

Calabretta gives me a confused look.

I glance back over and raise my eyebrows. What? I just want to cut them back down to size a bit. They're pissing me off with their big balls. Men with cars as weapons. They can cut that right out, in my opinion.

Two of the shiny-suited knights start to twitch slightly round the corners of their mouths. Aha. Noted. So, you two don't keep to the rules, got you.

How things are between me and the rules has got bugger all to do with you lot, incidentally.

Marcel Thomforde gets antsy.

'Shall we go and get a coffee somewhere? Then we're not disturbing anyone here. Er, if you're OK with not questioning me at the station.'

Silent nods on our part.

I think: this isn't an interrogation, why put it like that? He's covering his arse about something.

'I'd love to offer you all a cappuccino,' says Cardoso, 'but unfortunately our machine is out of order.'

Cappuccino.

Machine.

A ship'll sprout from Calabretta's head any second now.

'That's OK,' he says and smiles a leaden smile. 'There are loads of nice cafés here.'

We all turn towards the door at once, as if we're synchronised swimmers, and wait for Thomforde to grab his jacket.

Exit.

A hundred metres of four-lane traffic.

All these cars everywhere again.

All mouth and attitude now, but tomorrow morning they'll be bonfires somewhere.

In the end we land up at the kiosk where I got cardboard coffee and cigarettes the other day.

Thomforde looks a bit crumpled.

'Is this all right with you?'

'Sure,' I say, 'it's stopped raining now.'

Inspector Calabretta gets everyone a machine coffee, doesn't take long, there must be someone there today who knows how. And as the stuff wasn't brewed by Cardoso, it seems to be all right by Calabretta too.

If you put far too much sugar in it, it's OK anyway.

'We found a man's DNA in Nouri Saroukhan's car,' says Calabretta to Thomforde, who is stirring his coffee and visibly relaxing. 'Which of you was a regular passenger of his?'

Thomforde shakes his head. 'None of our colleagues got into Nouri's crummy Fiat. They hate small cars on principle. Apparently, they're for sissies.'

He lights a cigarette and takes a gulp of coffee.

'And even I found his car a bit naff, and I don't really care about that stuff when it's friends. We often hit the road together, but we always took my car.'

'Oh,' says Schulle, 'the Audi A6 Competition, is that yours?' He unpacks a smile from which every scrap of intelligence has gone astray within a single second. On Calabretta's face: the exact same thing.

Thomforde nods, with an expression that some people get when they're talking about puppies.

'Yes,' he says, 'but at home I drive an old Volvo.'

Schulle and Calabretta melt away, they're like wax in Thomforde's fleet.

I dream of a God who, at this very moment, would let the air out of the tyres of every car in our city.

'So that means,' I say, to bring the gentlemen back down to earth, 'that we'd be relatively unlikely to find genetic evidence of any of your colleagues in Nouri's car.'

Thomforde shrugs his shoulders. 'I'd say so, yes, relatively unlikely.'

'And if we were to find anything,' I say, 'the colleague concerned would presumably not have been in the car for professional reasons.'

Check me out, I sound so badass, like one of the hardcore pros from Verden an der Aller, man.

'Presumably not,' says Thomforde, pulling a face like he's also in just the mood to recreate a scene from *The Rockford Files*.

'You run two expensive motors?' asks Anne Stanislawski. 'I can't even afford to keep one decent car on the road.'

'The Audi's leased,' says Thomforde. 'But it's a pretty well-paying industry.'

'Nouri Saroukhan was saving for something,' says Brückner, 'if his bank statements and spartan flat are anything to go by. You don't happen to know what that could have been, do you?'

Thomforde shakes his head. 'Not a clue, money was something he never wanted to talk about somehow. Even though it's a permanent topic of conversation in insurance, everyone's always talking about who's splashed the cash again and on what, or who can afford what fancy holiday or membership of which exclusive club, or what lousy gas barbecue. None of that was at all important to Nouri. I think he kept his bank balance bulging to buy himself freedom and stay safe.'

He gulps his coffee, lights a cigarette, draws the smoke deep into his lungs, and then he says: 'I don't want to drop anyone in the shit. But...'

Aha. Got you. Now I understand why we're standing around outside this kiosk and why he put so much stress earlier on being 'questioned'. Thomforde wants to get something off his chest.

'But?' asks Calabretta. He turns his upper body towards Thomforde and pricks up his ears.

'Nouri wasn't stupid. He wasn't the kind of guy to crash out blind drunk in his car. And he didn't kill himself either. He was stable, and he had plans for his life. He was a cool guy.'

Thomforde looks around as if to check whether the coast is clear. Then he takes a deep breath in and out again and says quietly: 'One of my colleagues is acting weirdly. He looks kind of more nervous than normal.'

He drags on his cigarette again.

'And for him, that's pretty hard to beat.'

Here's something.

Here's some meat and potatoes.

We all feel it at once.

General twitching of neck muscles.

I light a cigarette for myself and look Thomforde in the eyes. 'Go on, please.'

'I have no idea what it's all about,' he says. His head slumps between his shoulders, now his courage seems to be deserting him. He thinks again about whether he really wants to go through with what he's resolved to do.

Calabretta gives him a little time and nurses his coffee as if there was nothing the matter. Then, very cautiously: 'Who are we talking about here?'

'Robin Noack,' says Thomforde. 'I think you should definitely talk to Robin Noack.'

Calabretta nods. Slowly and gently. 'Noack,' he says. 'OK. Now you mention him, he's totally shut us down, right from the start.'

'But if you grill him directly now,' says Thomforde, 'he'll know that I put you on to him, and then I might as well just quit.'

'Why so?' asks Anne Stanislawski.

'Robin knows that I like men. He once saw me at night on the street with a guy I know.'

'So?' I say. 'Where's the problem?'

'You really can't imagine this macho culture at AKTO, can you?' he asks. 'It's like in the army or a football team. They're afraid of gays.'

Oh, Lordy. The usual shit.

'Oh, man,' I say. 'What on earth are you doing in this place?'

The longer I look at Marcel Thomforde, the more urgent a single thought becomes in my mind: quit and work somewhere else. That joint'll bring you to your knees otherwise.

'I kind of drifted into it,' he says. 'And then if you quit you lose all the cash. That's hard. It's really good money.'

He takes a last drag on his cigarette, drops it and stamps it out.

'I'm only talking to you because I liked Nouri. But I don't want trouble.'

'We won't cause you any trouble,' I say. 'We'll think of something.'

'What's the average coke consumption in a place like that?' asks Brückner.

Thomforde briefly throws his head back and laughs, then he says: 'Man, what makes you ask that now...?'

'Well, if, for example, we had concrete suspicions of cocaine abuse,' I say, 'if, for example, we accidentally found something, we could then pass it relatively unbureaucratically to our colleagues on the drugs squad, and then they'd go in, and then we, in turn, could take a deep and very elegant look at your colleague's computers and files, what was his name again...?'

'Robin Noack,' says Calabretta.

Thomforde exhales audibly. He's passed us the ball. He's out.

And because that's probably a good feeling, he ups the ante.

'Robin snorts so much cocaine up his nose everyday I'm surprised it's still there. He must burn easily ten grams a week, and at the weekend he throws in the same amount again.'

'Whew,' says Anne Stanislawski, 'that's got to add up a bit.'

'About two thousand euros a week,' I say.

Brückner whistles through his teeth.

'So Noack probably has money problems,' says Calabretta.

'Almost certainly,' says Thomforde. 'He's currently trying to save his arse with online poker or something. But I think he's just plunging in deeper and deeper. I'm kind of sorry for him.'

'Would it be a problem for you personally if the guys came round with a couple of sniffer dogs?' asks Anne Stanislawski.

Old school. First protect your informant.

Thomforde shakes his head. 'No. I'm more the rum-and-Coke sort.'

All the same, I'm glad he didn't say 'prosecco on ice' because I wouldn't necessarily stake my life on the unfazed masculinity of *my* colleagues.

BAKING POWDER

It goes exactly as we'd expected. A whole three insurance agents donate us a little spit and thus their genetic code.

Marcel Thomforde, obviously.

The two who've lost their licences are on me – they wanted to make a good impression for once, just in case.

Boss Cardoso says: no. Where would it lead us?

Everyone else has a highly urgent need to get to his next meeting.

Calabretta has a highly urgent need to take a leak.

And while he's there, he peeks into this little cabinet where the gentlemen store cheap loo paper and expensive deodorant, and there he finds a little bag of white powder.

Just to be on the safe side, he prefers not to ask Messrs Insurance Agents if anyone is planning to bake a cake today, or if he can borrow their baking powder.

He just pockets it.

When we're outside again, he calls Brux, our colleague from drugs.

Let's see exactly where this leads us.

GIVE US THE PUNCHLINE, PLEASE

Faller wants to talk to us. Over a beer in the Blue Night.

I don't think I've ever been to the Blue Night for a beer. I've only ever been to the Blue Night for ten beers.

Stepanovic is on his third beer and I'm on my second when Rocktäschel and Lindner come in. Just after Stepanovic orders his fourth, the door opens and Faller's here.

Our two young colleagues are a bit wary of the place. There's no kind of design or art or DJ or whatever else going on that somehow pigeonholes the usual, rather newer pubs in St Pauli as part of the cultural mainstream. This is the deepest Kiez, even if the walls are repainted every couple of years. The new paint doesn't do anything to change the smell, the feel, the sound of this place. The Blue Night is perfectly off-beat, it makes a living from its core being broken away, from standing here on the edge with all its customers, wondering what's actually going on here.

Carla isn't here, and Calabretta is still barred, at least as far as Rocco goes.

'OK,' says Faller. 'I talked to a few people this afternoon, who are usually very well informed. There are no indications that your Mhallami families want to get into any kind of business here. There's practically nothing going down at all.'

He takes a swig from his beer bottle.

'They're not our Mhallami families,' says Rocktäschel, who has every right to be a little sensitive.

Faller gives him a look that's somewhere between prudent and askance, and sticks a cigarette in his mouth.

'And then there's the thing with the girl.'

Stepanovic furrows his brow and looks at me.

Did you...?

Yes, I did.

Ah. OK.

Sometimes I wonder if telepathy is actually something you learn in Frankfurt.

'What about the girl?' asks Stepanovic, giving Faller a light.

'I've heard that you're better off looking for her in the Schanze district than anywhere else.'

'And where did you hear that?'

'In a pub round the corner here,' says Faller, 'from one of the bar staff. She worked in Le Fonque for a while, and she reckoned she might have seen the girl there a few times.' He drags on his cigarette. 'Of course, she wasn't sure. You know how it goes. And then the photo's pretty old.'

'But then the face is sort of special, somehow,' says Stepanovic.

Faller studies the beer bottle in his hand. 'It certainly is.'

Then silence.

No Mhallami here apart from Aliza Anteli.

Stepanovic runs his hand over his face and puts his beer bottle down rather too forcefully on the bar, some slops over.

'Who the hell killed Nouri Saroukhan? Family or friends?'

Spontaneously, I'd be inclined to say: life, but I'd better not say that, Stepanovic hates getting stuck so it's wiser not to make silly jokes. Although it wasn't all that silly, and it wasn't actually meant to be funny.

'I'd bet on enemies,' says Faller.

Well now, that wasn't one whit better, was it?

'Well,' says Lindner, who has until now been holding fast to his beer with his usual blank and mildly uncertain air, 'I think that if we're not dealing with clan criminality here, it follows that it can only be someone from the immediate Saroukhan family circle, or else that we've got to focus a hundred and fifty per cent on conditions in that weird world of insurance...'

Stepanovic gives him an irritated look. 'Lindner?'

'Yes?'

'Give us the punchline, please.'

Rocktäschel takes a big gulp of beer. 'Officer Lindner only wanted to say that he hasn't a clue.'

Stepanovic: 'Thanks.'

Then we drink together and wait for the questions to finally drop below the horizon.

Later, when everyone's gone, my friend Ivo and I are still sitting at the bar, Rocco's polishing a few glasses, there's not much on, even the football season's basically over. Stepanovic has his arm around my shoulders, but it's OK, it feels as though he's only put his arm down on me.

Half an hour ago, he started asking Rocco for spirits, since when we've basically been drinking one vodka after the next, with maybe ten minutes at most between them. We started with Russian Cocaine shots, now we're just drinking the vodka as it is, but of course you never drink just like that, there's always a reason.

Rocco's drinking away the fact that Carla's away, which she clearly is, today at least.

Stepanovic is drinking away his fear of the dark, of loneliness, of flats.

I'll take whatever's left.

'So, what's up with the Turkish Travolta now?' asks Stepanovic between drinking and putting his glass back down.

'What d'you think's up with him? He's got one arm and a plan missing. But he's got a place where he can stay.'

I drink a vodka.

'That's something anyway.'

'That's more than either of us has.'

'I want to know if you love him,' says Stepanovic.

Oh shit.

I can't talk about that kind of stuff.

I can't even think about that kind of stuff.

Could I please have some more vodka, PDQ?

Rocco's already pouring it and glaring witheringly at Stepanovic. 'Hey, you really can't do that, dude.'

'I can do much more than that,' says Stepanovic, and he drinks his vodka even quicker than I do mine. 'For example, I can tell you something, Riley, that I've wanted to tell you for a long time, but it's somehow never been the right moment, oh, fuck, there are some things where it's just never the right moment, so anyway, listen up...'

'Give us the punchline,' I say.

He looks at me. 'Right.'

He drinks another vodka and stares into his empty glass.

'I'd die for you.'

'What?'

He puts the glass down, takes my face in his hands, from the corner of my eye I see the glass tip over.

'No matter who you love or don't love, no matter what a stony creature you are, no matter whether you want it or not, there's someone who loves you and, if necessary, I'll give you that in writing.'

'It's not necessary,' I say and I immediately feel sick.

'Good,' he says, 'so at least we've got that cleared up at last.'

He pulls me to him.

And I'd say he kisses me as if I were a boiled egg.

It takes a while.

But I start to feel better not worse.

Maybe it wasn't just a shot glass that tipped over, maybe there was something inside me, because there's something leaking in my heart.

'So,' says Stepanovic, when he's finished kissing me, and Rocco's frantically filling up more glasses than three people can stand. 'Nothing else can go wrong now.'

'Why can nothing else go wrong now?'

The world swims away from my eyes, I close them and give up. His voice is very close to my ear, the rest of him is holding me tight.

'Because now we're spit-brothers.'

CUT

Calabretta and Carla.

They're sitting side by side on a wall.

Across the Elbe, with a view of the port.

Calabretta's playing the guitar.

Carla's singing.

Fado.

They're not doing anything else.

They're not doing anything that wouldn't be OK.

But people still keep whispering.

As if it were a bad habit.

As if the two of them were a bad habit.

But it just is the way it is.

Eventually, it gets too cold on the wall, and they walk home through the Old Elbe Tunnel. Calabretta's got his guitar on his back and Carla's hand in his.

A star falls from heaven and a gull laughs itself silly, while in Mexico, Argentina and Brazil, the streets are burning.

THE BARMAN WOULD LIKE TO GET SHOT OF US PRONTO, BUT THAT'S UNDERSTANDABLE

'We've got to be patient now and talk to the right people,' Stepanovic says.

We've just been in Le Fonque, it was shortly after nine, the place had just opened. It smelled of beer and cigarettes, and there was a whiff of marijuana – I can't remember it ever having smelled different there. I like the joint, the consistent red light, the velvet, the deep sofas, the shining glasses and eyes, the beating hearts, the music like a shot in the head. Once, when I still had a smooth face, I came here from time to time to work on buggering it up.

The barman looked at the picture of Aliza and didn't dilly-dally about it, maybe because he wasn't in the mood for stress.

'Nice woman. She's been hanging around the Flora for at least ten years. I reckon she squats there. What do you want with her?'

'We need her help,' I said, and tried not to drop into the sofa to my left. The red light in Le Fonque had bundled up the tiredness of recent days and weeks and months, ah, come off it, of recent years, and wrapped it around my body. And the fact that the information we'd been after for days was now suddenly lying on the table must have unleashed a wave of relief within me: I probably relaxed briefly, and this is what I got for it. Now, the tiredness won't go away.

'Do you need anything else? One for the road perhaps?'

The barman wanted to get shot of us pronto, but that was understandable in some ways, no publican likes to have the authorities in the house.

'Yes,' Stepanovic said, 'two Czech pilsners, please.'

Now we're sitting on a bike rack outside the pub with two bottles of Staropramen, peeling the paper off the bottlenecks. The Rote Flora is only a stone's throw away, but we can't just slouch in there like it's no big deal. A cop, a prosecutor, a riot – it could turn out like that. It definitely wouldn't prompt Aliza Anteli to talk to us.

'Hasn't Rocktäschel got that musician girlfriend?'

'I've never talked to Rocktäschel about music,' I say, but knowing Stepanovic, he chats to his younger colleagues about all kinds of stuff.

'His girl,' he says. 'She plays the drums in some kind of underground band and, on the side, she dances burlesque in a punk-rock joint round here. Maybe she could put us in touch with someone.'

'Really?' I say. 'Rocktäschel's got a punk-rock girlfriend?'

'Yes,' Stepanovic says, 'why not? I did myself once. Punk-rock girlfriends are the best.'

He pulls out his phone and dials Lennart Rocktäschel's number.

OK.

So we won't actually call on the intelligence service to pay a visit to the Rote Flora, we'd rather go via a colleague's burlesque punk-rock girl. Stepanovic can be a real damn Kinder Surprise sometimes. But if he says so.

'Evening, Rocktäschel, Ivo here,' he says, 'could you let me have your girlfriend's number, please?'

BETTER INSIDE THE TENT PISSING OUT THAN OUTSIDE THE TENT PISSING IN

Half an hour later we're standing with Rocktäschel and his girl-friend, Dolores, outside the Rote Flora. Dolores is wearing a very short black skirt and no tights, a thick, dark-green hoodie and pink biker boots. Her bleached blonde hair is knotted up into an impressive tower.

'You guys wait here,' she says, and then she goes in.

Rocktäschel smokes and looks around, and I think that there's an awful lot that I don't know about him.

'I wonder how she'll do it,' says Stepanovic.

'Oh,' Rocktäschel says, 'there's only one negotiating tactic there, isn't there: "Maybe it's better to have them inside the tent pissing out than to have them outside the tent pissing in"?'

He drags on his cigarette, and from the way he does it, anyone could recognise him as a policeman, beats me why that is. It's got something to do with his attentive expression as he inhales.

'She'll explain that to them,' he says. 'And then they'll talk to us, about whatever they want to and can, because it's the quickest way of getting shot of us.'

'Nobody's intending to piss into the Flora's tent,' I say.

'Well, maybe not,' says Rocktäschel, 'but if I were them, I wouldn't be quite so sure about that.' He throws his cigarette away. 'I'm sure they'll just send someone out soon to launch the charm offensive.'

It takes a little while.

We watch the activity on the Schulterblatt. It's almost ten, the Schanzenpiazza is rammed with young people, they're wearing skinny trousers, pleated skirts, straightened hair, the women wagging their handbags, the men wagging their smartphones. They're holding colourful drinks or craft beers, mango-flavoured if the bottles are anything to go by. Their voices are managing to drown out all the music that floods the square, nobody is really listening to anything or anybody. They're perfect consumers, perfectly functioning cogs in this big wheel into which they were thrown as children. They work, they shop, they go out, they do all of them quite a lot, they keep the machine running and the machine is happy.

They don't fit the people behind us who've been trying to live a different life for almost thirty years. Who're trying out the alternative approach to the carelessness, to the party-porn and to the groomed bars right opposite them. Two ends of the line about twenty metres apart and the rest of the city is somehow trying to balance in the middle and not fall off. There's nothing to link the Flora and me, but I'm convinced that the day on which the Flora disappears will be a bad day. Because then the scales will have tipped in the wrong direction.

As if I were an expert on balance, I mean, please.

Dolores comes out again.

She's got someone with her.

A man in his early fifties, he's slim and has an angular face, he's got friendly, dark eyes and short, thick black hair. He's wearing grey jeans and a dark, threadbare cardigan from the nineties.

He holds out his hand and gives us an open, clear look. He must be the one who's used to being sent out.

'Dolores says you'd like to speak to a friend of mine?'

'Aliza Anteli is a friend of yours?' Stepanovic says.

The man nods.

There aren't even any introductions. They aren't important. Talking is important.

'Aliza isn't here,' says the man. 'Hasn't been for a couple of days.'

'Are you worried?' asks Stepanovic.

Rocktäschel and I stay in the background, Dolores has edged away round the nearest corner.

The man shakes his head. 'You don't need to worry about Aliza.'

'A friend of hers was murdered,' says Stepanovic, 'and she might be in danger.'

The man looks at us.

His expression is closing in.

He won't say anything else.

Because actually, he is worried.

Shit.

Gone wrong.

Stepanovic does the only thing left for him to do. He pulls one of his business cards out of his trouser pocket and gives it to the man.

'Please, if you speak to Aliza: We need her help. And we might be able to help her if she's in difficulties. Tell her to call us. All off the record, we'll meet her wherever she likes, we won't stick to the official script.'

The man stows the card away, nods to us again, then turns and disappears into the Rote Flora.

We watch him go; clouds build up in the sky.

'Debrief,' says Stepanovic.

Rocktäschel lights a cigarette and says: 'Went OK.'

THE ZOMBIE APOCALYPSE AT LAST

By taxi to the Police Museum.

There wasn't much to say and wasn't much to do, so we landed straight on the carpet.

Huge fireworks on all sides and anyone who isn't paying attention gets blown sky-high, and, oh, who needs love anyway when they can have ghost-pirate films?

NOURI AND ALIZA ON MEXICO STREET

She had something to do in the north of the city, she'd told Nouri – some campaign her friends were part of, but in truth it was to do with a passport for her. Some people from Greece were passing through on their way to Denmark for a campaign, and the Greeks knew their stuff when it came to papers. Apparently, they could take the right pictures, and they'd got Italian documents with them, proper documents. Aliza didn't know how the hell they did it, but it was a chance. Her friends had said it'd be good enough for a container ship across the Atlantic.

Aliza had spent the night at Nouri's and driven with him to City Nord, then later she'd go on to Steilshoop. Which was where the flat was where the Greeks were staying.

Nouri was dejected, he'd been dejected all night, something was weighing him right down, which was why she hadn't mentioned the papers to him just yet. She'd tell him when she'd got the papers. She'd lay them on his pillow.

She knew that he'd saved enough money for them both.

She knew that then they'd be able to leave any time.

All that was missing now was a ship.

They sat in his car and listened to music.

'What's up?' she asked. 'Is something up in Bremen?'

He shook his head. 'Bremen doesn't exist anymore,' he said,

but he knew that it was the other way around: he didn't exist for Bremen anymore, and that was basically fine by him.

'One of my colleagues is planning some kind of shit.'

'What's that to you?'

She'd had enough of men who were planning some kind of shit. She never wanted anything to do with men who were planning any kind of shit again, unless it was shit to do with her papers.

'He wants to con old people,' Nouri said. 'I accidentally over-heard him planning it.'

'Did you talk to him?'

'No. The guy's a coke-head and not all there.'

She reached into her long curls and twiddled them. The curls were so soft. When they were in Mexico, she'd shave her hair off. And then her curls would grow again, soft, black curls.

'Then tell your boss.'

He shook his head and wound up the window; he was cold. 'He's also a coke-head and not all there. I don't trust him. He might even be in on it.'

He turned the radio knob, looking for a different station.

'Crap music.'

On the news they said that cars had been burning again in Hamburg overnight.

'Is it your guys doing that, by the way?'

She shook her head, but she wasn't entirely certain. After all, everyone did what they wanted.

She thought the phrase again, and found it pleasing.

'If the stuff with this colleague is depressing you this much, you've got to do something, Nouri.'

She didn't want him to bring it with him when they went. She wanted them to be able to forget everything and be free.

'I know one of the old ladies he wants to rip off,' he said. 'If he does it, she'll have nothing left. I've made up my mind to talk to him. I've written to him. I wrote that I want to talk to him. That I know he's about to land himself in the shit. I've told him that I'll be here soon. If he doesn't come, I'll call the cops.'

She thought: I don't know.

She said: 'OK. Let me know, yeah?'

She didn't have a good feeling.

She'd stay close by until he got in touch.

'How about you?'

She'd have liked to have told him that Mohamed was running around Hamburg showing people a photo of her. She'd heard about it. Apparently, it wasn't a very good photo, it was fuzzy and taken from a distance, but it was a recent picture, and you could recognise her. She had no idea where he'd got the picture from, but she knew she shouldn't mention it to Nouri now. One thing at a time, and then they'd see.

'Everything's going fine for now,' she said. 'Maybe soon we'll get aboard a ship and then we'll be out of here.'

'As stowaways?'

'We already are.'

MRS HALFMANN, MRS BOURDIEU AND MR GIESE

Brux and his drugs guys waited a day for the sake of propriety and then joined in with our little game. In the end, a call from Stepanovic and a piece of printed paper from me were enough.

Between them, seven desk drawers at AKTO gave up eighty grams of cocaine, and clearly nobody had dusted the toilet recently.

The boss himself had almost twenty grams in his drawer, while around ten grams was found in each of the other six desks, as befits a functioning hierarchy.

Robin Noack was not in the office.

Cardoso flipped.

The computers and files were all provisionally confiscated on suspicion of professional drug dealing. We know that we won't be able to keep the stuff for long – AKTO's lawyers are already up in arms – so we sit in our incident room with Brux and his three men and look through it all. It's a pressure cooker. Nobody's talking, some of us have forgotten to breathe. We don't expect to find anything to do with drug dealing, we're looking for something else, even if we don't know exactly what. But there must be something somewhere. Just a hint. Maybe even one pointing towards Robin Noack.

The frantic hustling through files and computers is almost as tiring as my life.

Until Anne Stanislawski finds something on the system, and suddenly nobody's yawning.

'Hang on a mo,' she's just said quietly, with a frown, and now she says: 'Three life insurance policies on Robin Noack's customer list matured in the last few weeks.'

She pulls the laptop she's sitting at closer to her and scrolls down a bit.

'The money was paid out too, and not to three different accounts, but only to two. Could somebody pass me a cigarette?'

I light one and hand it to her, while she flicks through a file that's lying on the desk next to the laptop. She runs her fingers down the columns on the paper, drags on her cigarette and coughs. She doesn't even smoke, does she?

'Sorry,' she says, amid her bronchial rumbling, 'I normally only smoke after dark.'

She keeps her index finger resting on the paper and her brow furrowed.

'Here. Right...'

She coughs again.

'I'll eat my hat if Mrs Emilie Halfmann and Mr Otto Giese, who live in separate old people's homes on opposite sides of the city, have a joint account at Targo Bank.'

Targo Bank. Calabretta reaches for the telephone and says: 'Account number?'

Stanislawski dictates the number; he writes it on his pad.

'Chief Inspector Vito Calabretta, Hamburg CID, could you please tell me the holder of the following account number...?'

The bank official must be squirming.

'Or we could swing by,' Calabretta says, 'a whole squad of us. If you'd prefer.'

He wouldn't prefer.

He looks something up for us.

'OK, thanks.'

Calabretta hangs up. 'Robin Noack.' He looks at me. 'We need to get into his account asap. And we need a search warrant for his place.'

'I'll get them for you,' I say. 'How about the second account?'

Anne Stanislawski says: 'Deutsche Bank. The life insurance for a Mrs Lisette Bourdieu was paid into it.'

She reaches for the receiver, same game as Calabretta and Targo Bank just now, except that this bank clerk seems to talk a fraction more quickly. She hangs up again.

'Robin Noack.'

'A hit,' says Stepanovic, looking towards the murder squad. 'Will you drive out to see Mrs Halfmann, Mrs Bourdieu and Mr Giese, and talk to the ladies and gentleman about their insurance agent? Riley, shall I give you a lift back to your office so you can get down to work? We need to get into Noack's accounts. And into his flat too.'

NOBODY CAN HELP ME

We're driving down Rothenbaumchaussee, and the Mercedes is squealing its heart out, when Stepanovic's phone rings. He hands it to me.

Number withheld.

'Could you get it?'

I hold the telephone to my ear. 'Stepanovic's phone, Riley speaking.'

'This is Aliza Anteli.'

I almost drop the handset.

'Hello, Ms Anteli.'

Stepanovic takes his foot off the gas and pulls over. The Mercedes jolts over the curb before it comes to a stop.

'It's good of you to ring,' I say, and hope that she doesn't notice the synapses that just shorted in my brain. Stepanovic grips the wheel and looks at me wide-eyed.

'Do you need our help?'

She doesn't answer immediately. Then she says quietly: 'I heard you needed my help.'

'Where are you, Ms Anteli?'

'In a phone box,' she says, 'don't bother.'

'District?'

'Nice try.'

'We'd like to meet you. We're in the car, just tell me where you are and we'll come.' I add: 'If we can help you in any way.'

I've given Stepanovic my phone, he gets out of the car and is presumably calling the tech guys so that they can try to trace the call as fast as possible.

'Nobody can help me,' she says, and her voice cracks.

There are a few seconds of silence.

'Ms Anteli? Are you still there?'

'It was my brother.'

Question mark.

'Your brother?'

'Yes,' she says, 'Mohamed.'

'What was Mohamed?'

'Mohamed killed Nouri.'

Stepanovic has just slid back into his seat and I can see how he's breathing.

'Ms Anteli, both your brothers have an alibi for the night Nouri died.'

'It was him, I swear. Beats me how he did it, but he's got Nouri on his conscience. The way our shitting families have us both on their consciences. Fucking twats, the lot of them.'

'You think your brother set Nouri's car on fire?'

'My brother's set heaps of cars on fire.'

Another pause. She seems to be looking for her voice.

'And if he finds me, he'll set me on fire too.'

'Once again, Ms Anteli: we can help you, if you let us.'

'You can shove your lousy witness protection up your arses, it just doesn't work.'

Right.

I try again.

'Has your brother threatened you?'

She laughs. Briefly and bitterly. It's more of a cough.

'My brother's threatened me since the moment I was born.'

The laugh has gone.

'He's looking for me. Everyone's looking for me. And now you're looking for me too. D'you understand?'

'We're not looking for you, we—'

'Oh, give it a rest.'

Click.

Stepanovic and I breathe in and then out again.

I give him his phone back and light us cigarettes.

'This is nuts,' I say. 'She insists her brother Mohamed killed Nouri. But it was all a bit confused.'

'No wonder,' Stepanovic says. 'If I were her, I'd have landed up in the nut house long ago.'

'Where did she call from?'

'Phone box in Steilshoop.'

'Damn it,' I say, 'that's too far. Search party?'

Stepanovic shakes his head. 'The woman's living permanently on the run. I don't want to be chasing her too. She's done us no harm.'

I give him a sideways glance and something warm calls round. He shoves the cigarette into the corner of his mouth and turns the car key in the ignition.

It sticks a little bit but he's not giving up.

When the Mercedes is finally rolling, he says: 'So. I'll drive you to your office. And on the way, you can call Bargfrede in Bremen, tell him to take a team round to the Antelis' and have a firmer word with Mohamed Anteli. If his sister is that convinced it was him, there's got to be something in it. Bugger the alibis.'

SHE'S A LYING WHORE

'Which sister?' asks Mohamed Anteli, and as he speaks, his chin shoots forwards. He's sitting on a chair, legs wide, shoulders wide, arms crossed over his chest, he barely fits into the chair. His black beard glistens, so does his shaved head, but differently.

'Your sister Aliza,' says DCI Bargfrede.

'Can kiss my arse, and so can pissing Melika.'

'Aliza says you've got Nouri Saroukhan on your conscience.'

'Course she says that. 'Cos she talks nothing but shit. And what's that to you, copper? I was in jail that night, you know that.'

'You've got friends.'

'I have family.'

'You've got people you could send.'

'Where?'

'To Hamburg. To bump off the Saroukhans' son.'

'Saroukhan. *Pff.*'

'You're angry, Mr Anteli.'

'Shut it.'

'Be careful, yeah?'

'I'll talk how I like.'

'Ismail Saroukhan and his sons talk how they like, Mr Anteli. You don't. Shame, huh?'

Mohamed Anteli breathes it away, the sword that's sitting in his throat, that he'd like to draw, and then he'd bisect them all with his sword, the sharpest and longest of them all, that's how he sees it.

'Why does your sister think you killed Nouri Saroukhan?'

'How should I know? She's a lying whore. She's lied since the day she was born. And now she's lying again. She needs to stop lying.'

'Have you spoken to her?'

A laugh gone wrong, a choke, a cough.

'She's got no time for me, copper. Because she just had to run crying to you. And now piss off out of my house.'

'We're not in your house, Mr Anteli. This house belongs to the Saroukhans.'

'Fuck-all belongs to them!'

Tarik Anteli sits next to his big brother in silence. He pulls a face like someone's cut his tongue out.

HAMBURG – MOSCOW – BANGKOK

It's early afternoon, nobody had lunch, we're sitting together in our squad office being hungry. But there's no food, there's something to discuss.

Calabretta's just been to Robin Noack's flat with Anne Stanislawski, a couple of uniformed colleagues and a search warrant. Schulle and Brückner are still out at the respective banks with the warrants for the accounts, but they should be back soon.

Lying on the table are various print-outs of movement data from Noack's mobile phone. And photos from his flat. They include one of an open, virtually empty wardrobe.

On Stepanovic's phone, on loudspeaker: Bremen. Bargfrede is telling us about the recent, and predictably far from satisfactory, questioning of Mohamed Anteli, and I get the impression that this time it annoyed him more than usual. He sounds pissed off, and he says that the two Anteli brothers will be watched round the clock from now on. He'd also like to put the Saroukhan men from Nouri's family under surveillance, but right now, unfortunately, he doesn't have the staff to watch them round the clock and, because he thinks there's something brewing at the Antelis' right now, an observation there might be more useful; Mohamed was ready to blow.

Rocktäschel lobs the Batman idea into the mix again.

We all still like it, but it doesn't get us any further.

We help ourselves to the sheets with the printed-out movement data and look at them.

'On the morning of Nouri Saroukhan's death, Robin Noack was in City Nord,' says Calabretta, 'at five twenty-six a.m. But, and this sucks, the time alone isn't enough to pin the crime on him – Saroukhan could have been given the roofies hours earlier. But on the other hand, the car was torched around half past five.'

'Ah, come on, it was him,' says Anne Stanislawski.

I think she's just had enough of this.

'Saroukhan found out about the dodgy dealings with the life insurance and was going to squeal. So he had to go.'

'That's probably exactly what happened,' Stepanovic says, looking through the phone data. 'But where's the guy got to now? His phone's been off since last night; before that, it was still in his flat.'

'He hasn't turned up at the office since yesterday,' says Anne Stanislawski, 'and the flat in Winterhude is empty, hardly any clothes, no suitcases.'

'Airport,' says Stepanovic.

Calabretta glances at Stanislawski, and she says: 'I'm on it.'

She reaches for the telephone, jams the receiver to her ear and grabs a notepad and pen in passing.

'How about the port,' I say. 'Container ships?'

OK, that's how I'd do it if I were Robin Noack, I'd already be on a ship to Curaçao with the dosh, but I think I'm a different type.

'God forbid,' says Calabretta, 'what a can of worms.'

He stops breathing because he knows that you can't seal off a massive port and you can't monitor it, and he stares at

Stanislawski, who's just got through to the right office at Hamburg airport. She rattles off her Hamburg CID bit, listens, nods, hangs up, and says: 'We're in luck. Robin Noack is intending to fly to Bangkok via Moscow at quarter to six this evening. Or he checked in online, at least.'

'Please God, don't let him change his mind and take a ship after all,' says Calabretta.

'He'll turn up,' says Stepanovic as he positions himself at the open window and lights a cigarette.

Calabretta's phone rings.

Schulle and Brückner are on the line.

Robin Noack withdrew a total of almost 600,000 euros from his accounts this morning, in cash. The 150,000 at Deutsche Bank were supposedly for a new Porsche, the 448,000 at Targo Bank were to buy a flat. The vendor wanted it in cash, he told the bank clerks when they enquired.

And because he always handled a lot of cash, they actually believed him.

Give me a break.

These days, 450,000 won't buy you a flat that a piece of puke like Robin Noack would even set foot in.

YOU NEVER FORGET HOW

There are five of us. Calabretta, Stepanovic, Brückner, Anne Stanislawski and me. Plus four extensively armed colleagues from the airport police. It's nearly five.

We've been waiting for half an hour for Noack to pass through security. Ten minutes ago, we heard from luggage check-in: he's checked in his cases, two large ones. So he'll come. And, clearly, he's not expecting us.

The security cameras are transmitting pictures to the airport guys' screens. Robin Noack is tall and has exaggeratedly broad shoulders – he's the kind of guy who only pumps up his upper body in the gym. His hair cut is short and snappy, his face is almost a little too soft and boyish, and his head is too small for that robust body: something's not adding up here. His smile at the woman behind the desk is somewhat wired, but very friendly. Like someone who's just really looking forward to his holiday.

'Here we go,' says Calabretta.

Three minutes later, Robin Noack places a mobile phone, a wallet and a leather belt in a blue plastic crate, and pops the crate on the conveyor belt.

'All right,' say our four colleagues with the guns.

We're standing next to a grey plastic screen, the CID and I are hiding behind the uniformed guys, who are just standing around as normal. We've got a good view and we're hoping to blend in.

A security man waves Robin Noack into the body scanner. He stands still for a moment, adopts the scanner pose, then walks almost straight towards us.

'Nab him,' says Stepanovic quietly, and the guys nab him, Calabretta and Stanislawski draw their guns and cover the guys, Stepanovic covers everything else.

I look on at it all and think: flawless arrest. Robin Noack lay on his belly for a whole five seconds, now he's standing up again, and his hands are on his back in handcuffs.

You never forget how, eh, gentlemen.

Then the whole baggage train makes its way to an interview room that the guys here have got ready.

Robin Noack swears like a navvy.

WHAT, NO COKE?

A table with two chairs: sitting on one side is Robin Noack, sitting on the other side are Calabretta and Brückner. Robin Noack is sweating and sniffing.

Looks like there's something up with him, but I think it's more that there isn't anything up, and that's what's wrong with him.

Two of the airport police secure the door from the inside, Anne Stanislawski has stayed outside and is informing the rest of the squad, Stepanovic and I are leaning against the wall and acting like we're not here. The cold wall at my back and the milky light falling through the opaque windows draw the fatigue from my subconscious to the surface. I could fall asleep standing up. Let's see, I think, and my eyelids flutter.

'Where is the money?'

Noack sniffles.

'What money?'

'The six hundred thousand euros from Mrs Halfmann, Mrs Bourdieu and Mr Giese, with which you were intending to abscond to Thailand.'

'I don't know what you mean.'

He leans back, but his spine immediately jerks forwards again, as if there were an electric current running through the chairback. He does it twice in a row. The current must actually be coming from within.

It's amazing how well I can relax with all this fidgeting. But something's just pulled the plug on me. I topple a little in Stepanovic's direction, until my shoulder touches his, then I exhale rather too loudly. Calabretta heard, but he takes it in his stride. No surprise there. That guy's got nerves of steel. And my nerves seem to have been steel-plated too, because they don't let the crucial interrogation of a key suspect put them off their stride, and their stride pattern says: that's enough now. I slip a little further down against Stepanovic, he applies counter-pressure, it feels like: you're all right now. And then it feels like I'm falling asleep, and maybe it isn't just a feeling.

I can't do any more.

I can't do a thing except sleep standing up against a wall.

I don't know whether my eyes are open or closed.

I hear.

The coke.

The money.

The poker.

Who, what, why?

There's a fog in my head.

Some of it's got into my ears too.

Nouri.

That wasn't me.

What roofies?

Leave me alone.

I want to go.

I'm leaving now.

My plane's leaving.

Can I go to the toilet.

What, no coke.

I don't even know this Nouri.

This is all a big misunderstanding.

Lawyer.

Now I really do have to.

I.

Have.

To.

No.

Telephone.

Threw it away.

Car key.

Threw it away.

Help me.

Please.

I.

It was.

Shit.

It's only when Robin Noack breaks down completely that I come round; my senses are back in the game.

He's crying, he's sweating, he's beating his hands against his forehead, it's the coke that isn't up, he needs it so badly but it's left him in the lurch. Everything's gone, gone wrong, there's only a weight that's now crushing him. He stammers, he spits words out, there's a sentence at the end: 'And then I set him on fire.'

The old people's money is with Western Union in Bangkok.

I slide down the wall and stay sitting on the floor while Calabretta and Stepanovic pull Robin Noack off his chair and drag him away as if he were a wet sack of cement.

WE'LL TAKE OVER AT STILLHORN

Later, when the sun's hanging as low over the horizon as if it were about to crash, Stepanovic, Rocktäschel and I are standing outside the police HQ and eating chips. Lindner is upstairs with the others: they're writing reports.

'Burning cars outside the UN in New York,' says Rocktäschel, who's reading the news on his phone, and I say: 'No way.'

We're not talking much because it's better that way.

Each of us would rather lose ourselves in our own thoughts for a bit.

Stepanovic hasn't yet said a word about me falling asleep.

His phone rings, he licks his fingers and answers it.

It's Bargfrede.

Stepanovic puts it on speaker.

'Hello, Bargfrede, what's up?'

'Mohamed Anteli's evidently on the way to Hamburg, he's heading east on the A1. Two of our officers are right on his tail, they're just outside Sittensen. Just in case that's of any interest to you.'

'That's very interesting,' says Stepanovic. 'Can I have your two colleagues' numbers? We'll take over at the Stillhorn services.'

ALIZA AND THE FIRE

She had gone away because she thought: what's the worst that could happen? But then the uneasy feeling had turned bad: she suddenly knew that something had happened, at any rate, and she'd rather make an idiot of herself or cramp Nouri's style than not be there if he needed her.

She'd come over the rooftops; first she wanted to see what was going on, just wanted to keep an eye on things. The people from Greece would wait another half-hour for her. They needed the cash she had in her bag to get them to Copenhagen.

They'd wait.

It took a moment before she realised that the car was burning. And that Nouri was in it.

She pulled her telephone from her bag and called the fire brigade, short and sharp; she'd got a grip on herself, her stocks of despair had been used up long ago.

Then she hung up and ran down to the street, six floors she ran down.

She rattled the driver's door, the door was locked, she banged on the window, she hammered on the windscreen, she shook the whole car, but nothing worked.

She looked for a stone that she could smash the windscreen with.

She couldn't find one.

She couldn't even find an iron bar, for fuck's sake.

Nouri wasn't moving.

The interior filled with smoke.

She heard sirens. The fire brigade.

She placed a hand on the car roof, she said: 'Hang in there.'
Then she ran back up to the roof and waited.

She saw them cut the car open and pull him out. She saw
them do things to him, more people coming, more and more,
doctors, police, a woman in a trench coat.

She saw them put Nouri in an ambulance and drive away.

She saw the woman walk away and come back, she saw them
drinking coffee and smoking and talking, and then she saw that
they'd seen her.

She vanished across the roof.

Whoever might have set Nouri on fire, she knew one person
who definitely knew how: Mohamed.

Grief turned to rage, rage turned to hate.

The rage had always been there. Now there was hate.

Perhaps she didn't need papers anymore, but what she definitely did need was a gun.

SHUT YOUR GOB, BITCH

She must have enticed him here. At any rate, they seem to be expecting each other. The sun's just gone down, the dusk is swallowing up the contours.

Aliza Anteli is standing on the roof of the car park on Mexico Street, staring at the car that's just arrived. Her brother drove straight up to the top level and hasn't got out yet as we scurry, hush, hush, hush, quietly up the stairs.

We drop to the ground and slide the last little bit on our bellies from the door to a steel wall that's about a metre high and has a little gap for people to walk through.

There's nothing else here for people, everything's made of concrete. Stepanovic and Rocktäschel have drawn their guns. We can't see the brother and sister, we can only hear them.

It's not enough.

Stepanovic nods to Rocktäschel to slide back to the door. Position himself behind the door frame, hide there and keep everything in sight.

The darkness is playing into our hands.

Rocktäschel crawls, cat-like, and then has a position with a view.

Stepanovic and I have ears.

The car door opens.

Mohamed Anteli sniffs. He's a giant.

'My so-called sister.'

'Mo.'

'Don't call me Mo, it's disrespectful. You have to respect me, you whore.'

Aliza doesn't answer.

I watch Rocktäschel.

Rocktäschel's watching Aliza. Playing around his mouth is that particular twist that people get in the second they forget about a worry or a pain. I think he's smiling a bit, but I don't think he's even noticed.

I think it's OK.

'What do you want, sister?'

'Have you forgotten my name?'

'I don't give a shit about your name. I don't give a shit about you. You've brought shame on us all. You've dragged our family's honour through the dirt. You stink.' He sniffs like an ox again. 'Come on, what do you want, I haven't got time for this.'

'So why did you come then?'

'What. Do. You. Want.'

'I want to ask you something.'

'Intriguing.'

'Why did you kill Nouri?'

'Saroukhan? That wimp? I wouldn't dirty my hands on *him*.'

'You're lying. You killed him because you want to kill me.'

'I was in jail when he died, sister.'

'You were here, Mo.'

'I haven't even got a car.'

'So what's that?'

'Belongs to my dentist.'

'Then was it your dentist?'

'Maybe. Or maybe it was the devil.'

'You don't scare me anymore, Mo.'

'Pity. That's really why I came. I wanted to see you cry again.'

His voice is getting more and more cutting.

We ought to tackle them now.

Rocktäschel? He's perfectly calm. Relaxed.

Stepanovic seems turned to stone, he's not moving.

Maybe it's Aliza's voice. She sounds like a chain-smoking mermaid. A siren for specific requirements.

'You want to hurt me? Guess what, I figured that out. But you can't anymore. Where did you get the photo of me you were traipsing round Hamburg with?'

'So you heard about that?'

'Where did you get the photo?'

'Maybe from a friend who works for one of the security firms at the port? You and that limp dick were always meeting there. And then you...' he puts on a little-old-lady voice '... talked.'

He laughs. His laugh is so sharp you could cut something on it.

'That was probably all he was up to. Saroukhan.'

He spits.

'Stop it, Mo.'

'Or maybe it was your arsehole boyfriend himself who passed me the picture. Who knows?'

'Shut your gob, Mo.'

'Shut *your* gob, bitch.'

From the corner of my eye, I see something happening in Rocktäschel's face. He raises his eyebrows, his face suddenly brightens right up, as if he were glowing from inside.

Then a metallic click.

Then a laugh.

Mohamed Anteli laughs again, but the laugh isn't quite as sharp this time. Something's landed on the blade.

'What are you doing with that pop-gun, bitch...?'

Rocktäschel doesn't move, then he lowers his gun; Stepanovic springs up and points his P99 at Aliza, he shouts: 'Ms Anteli! Drop the gun! Police!'

But there's already been a bang, I stay put and stare at Rocktäschel, who's breathing and smiling, and then there are three, four more bangs, and then it's quiet, and then I hear the hard clatter of metal on concrete.

I stand up slowly.

Aliza's dropped the gun and is looking at Rocktäschel, who takes a step forwards and emerges from the darkness.

And then she walks slowly backwards.

Mohamed Anteli is lying beside his car, in a puddle of blood, he's not moving.

'Aliza,' I say, 'stay where you are.'

She looks from Rocktäschel to us and back again, and keeps walking backwards.

'Why don't you shoot?'

Stepanovic shakes his head.

Aliza takes another step.

And step.

By step.

By step.

Her face is pale, her hair seems to be ablaze.

'Aliza,' I say again, 'please.'

Rocktäschel stops, stretches a hand out to Aliza and says: 'That was nicely done.'

I wonder whether Rocktäschel's got a screw or two loose or whether the exact opposite is the case, whether he's got a fresher head than any of us, because, ultimately, that's true: Aliza Anteli did everything right.

I'd have done exactly the same.

At that moment, a storm breaks.

The storm comes from the left, from where the nearest high-rise borders the car park or, then again, maybe it comes from above, I can't pin it down, everything happens too quickly – the storm comes in the form of five women in black. Even their heads are swathed in black, they've got scarves tied round their faces, you can only see their eyes, they glint like cats' eyes in the darkness, their feet and hands fly through the air, they move so rapidly that none of us gets what's going on, there's a thud, then there's a jab, jab, jab, it's an ambush, first Stepanovic hits the ground, then Rocktäschel, then it's my turn, oh, wow, harsh, I think.

Everything goes black.

I'm falling.

And: silence.

Silence.

CRACKS IN THE SKY

Stepanovic says my name. He's lying on his stomach beside me, he's propped himself up on his elbows and rubbing his temples. There's a little blood running out of his mouth, might be a tooth in there too.

'Ninjas,' he says.

'Right,' I say. 'Ninjas.'

Rocktäschel groans and says: 'Fuck's sake, girls. We'd have let her go anyway.'

Maybe, I think, but it doesn't matter anyway now.

Aliza Anteli is gone.

Mohamed Anteli is dead.

My breastbone's weighing on me, my right shoulder's burning, my head's hammering. Above us, a couple of gulls are circling and screaming things, and it seems to me that they aren't just addressed to me, but to the whole damn world.

To our left, there's a crack in the sky.

THANKS to...

Karen Sullivan, for believing so passionately in books (and in me)

Rachel Ward, for always capturing and loving my sound

West Camel, for editing with brain and heart

Steph Broadribb, for adding Ninjas

Werner Löcher-Lawrence, Thomas Halupczok, Nora Mercurio

Gerald von Foris, for your good work at thirty-four degrees in the shade

The Hamburg Police Museum, for that one night

The Bremen Police Press Office

Thomas Ganz of the Lower Saxony State Office of Criminal Investigation, and the Lower Saxon CID in general, especially their inner courtyard

Dr Ralph Ghadban

Andreas Bonnet

Charly, for the time

Johnny and Daniel, for the drinks and the place

Karenina Köhler, I kiss your hand and blow you a kiss

Sonja Schäfer, for the money-laundering department

Romy and Wilhelm, for the internal compass

Domenico and Rocco: you know.